WHAT THE CROW SAID

THE UNIVERSITY OF ALBERTA PRESS

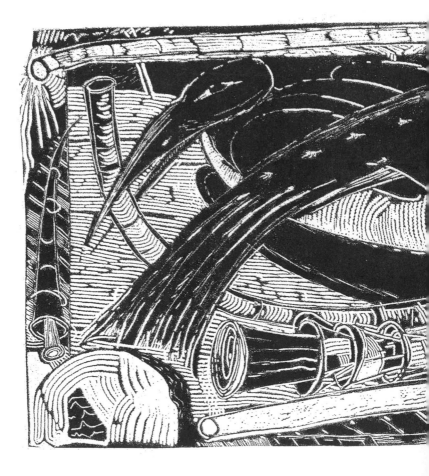

What the Crow Said

ROBERT KROETSCH

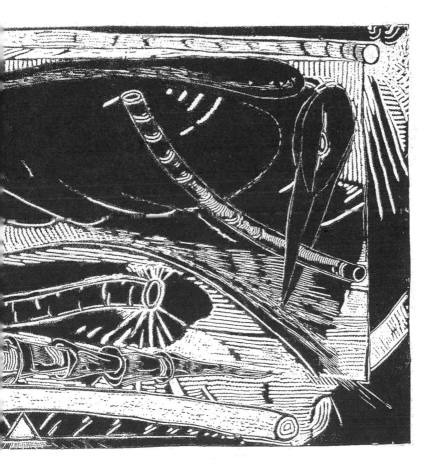

This edition published by
  The University of Alberta Press
  141 Athabasca Hall
  Edmonton, Alberta, Canada T6G 2E8

Printed in Canada 5 4 3 2 1
Text copyright © Robert Kroetsch 1978
Introduction copyright © Robert R. Wilson 1998
The back flap constitutes an extension of this copyright page.

CANADIAN CATALOGUING IN PUBLICATION DATA

  Kroetsch, Robert, 1927-
    What the crow said
    ISBN 0-888864-303-9

    I. Title.
    PS8521.R7W5 1998   C813'.54   C98-910861-9
    PR9199.3.K7W5 1998

ISBN 0–88864–303–9
A volume in (cuRRents), an interdisciplinary series. Jonathan Hart, series editor.

Printed and bound in Canada by Friesens, Altona, Manitoba.
∞ Printed on acid-free paper.

THE CANADA COUNCIL | LE CONSEIL DES ARTS
FOR THE ARTS | DU CANADA
SINCE 1957 | DEPUIS 1957

The University of Alberta Press gratefully acknowledges the support received for its publishing
program from the Canada Council for the Arts. In addition, we also gratefully acknowledge the
financial support of the Government of Canada through the Book Publishing Industry
Development Program for our publishing activities.

In Robert Kroetsch's fiction, everything in nature — winter sunshine or spring snowstorms — contains the embryos of human desire. A novel very much about desire, usually in startling manifestations, *What the Crow Said* must be read with a readiness to encounter many surprises. There are three fundamental levels in the novel (not exhausting its complexity) which the reader can never ignore. First, it is a novel about Alberta, rich in historical detail, its pages crowded with evocative images of landscape and rural life. Second, it is a fabulous novel, a fiction that goads imagination to work beyond the limits of historical truth and actual life. On this level, the reader continuously encounters strange events, unexpected warps to "ordinary" reality and characters who, like Jerry Lapanne (who builds an airplane to break out from prison but neglects, in his eagerness to escape, to give it the capacity to land), possess accomplishments that breach the boundaries of likelihood. Third, *What the Crow Said*, at once realistic and fantastic, constantly explores the possibilities of in-between spaces, of indeterminate places and moments in which apparently improbable events, experiences beyond the ordinary yet also partly within the realm of the familiar, take place with the simple persistence of wind and snow, human yearnings and aversion.

In Kroetsch's in-between spaces very ordinary things occur, but they do so with a twist, often quite simple in itself, that makes them seem momentarily aberrant, often deeply strange. It is as if one were to look at something quite commonplace in itself, familiar from hundreds of dealings, but were to do so through a magnifying-glass, the wrong end of a telescope, a prism, lenses of coloured glass, or "the convexity of encasing ice." Ordinary things would appear distorted, stretched into strange proportions, made unfamiliar. Take, for example, the War Against the Sky that erupts towards the end of the novel. Weather that perplexes, that defies both historical records and forecasts, that wearies patience and makes the mind yearn for a change, is familiar enough in Alberta. A person may wish for a change, suspect malevolence, shake an impotent fist, or curse beneath the breath; but Gus Liebhaber borrows Isador Heck's circus cannon (with which he had planned to shoot himself into heaven), steals Vera Lang's 576 hives of new bees, and attempts to fight back by firing bundles of bees into the sky. There is nothing unimaginably impossible about this act, although it may well seem strange in its intensity (Gus thinks he "would fertilize the barren sky") as well as in its misconception about the ways in which weather actually works. It becomes magical only when the bees return in stormy weather, in rain and hail: "Often, inside a huge hailstone, was a bee, frozen into perfect stillness, magnified by the convexity of the encasing ice." The in-between spaces of *What the Crow Said*, its indeterminate and conflicted areas, focus the potential of the ordinary.

In *What the Crow Said*, the collective and unnamed narrator recounts the shared experience of the town of Big Indian, which is located along an ambiguous borderline between Alberta and Saskatchewan. Big Indian is so remote from the rest of Alberta that it is possible for some of its inhabitants to doubt that anything exists beyond the borders of their municipality. The novel begins, in a burst of local detail and fabulous incident, when Vera Lang goes to a coulee along the Bigknife River one early spring day and takes off her clothes to luxuriate in the fresh crocuses, buffalo beans, violets, buttercups, and shooting stars. As she stirs awake from her dreaming, she is raped by a swarm of homeless bees. Her cry, "almost human," is heard in the town. It is terrified and "prolonged, but not a cry for help; despairing and ecstatic too." From that moment the sky "took umbrage" against the inhabitants of Big Indian, and a series of strange, even fantastic, events begins to unfold, all of which are connected in some way to the initial rape.

Following Vera's rape, there is a June blizzard in which her father, Martin Lang, freezes to death, although he remains, as a ghost, throughout the narrative. Eventually, Vera bears a son, whom she later throws to pursuing wolves (an act that may symbolize her transformed, bee-like nature). The son reappears later, having been raised by coyotes, speaking a bizarre language of his own. Vera's mother, Tiddy, is courted, like Homer's Penelope, by many suitors from all over the district. Two are especially important: John Skandl, the local ice merchant who expresses his love for her by building a lighthouse made of blocks of ice, and Gus Liebhaber, the local printer who possesses the uncanny ability to remember the future (he remembers Martin Lang's death but cannot prevent it). Although Tiddy marries Skandl, it is never clear that the son she bears is actually his and not Liebhaber's. That son, JG, is born physically perfect, the most beautiful child anyone in Big Indian has ever seen, but lacks the power of speech. He spends his life walking in figure eights and communicating with a crow who talks; he dies trying to imitate the crow by walking off the top of a tree. One pivotal event in the narrative is a card game, a game of schmier, that lasts 151 days and includes the ghost of Martin Lang among the players. Like the game of schmier, the events of *What the Crow Said* combine ordinary and fantastic elements. The anonymous, collective narrative voice invariably recounts them in a dry, matter-of-fact tone that neither seeks nor offers explanations. A reader may experience the novel as strange, an often-puzzling distortion of Alberta, but never as incoherent or "wrong." The strangeness of the narrative is Kroetsch's lens, the instrument of magnification that reveals hidden significance, itself no odder or more puzzling than human dreams, yearnings, and desire.

Although *What the Crow Said* has often been cited as an example of "magical realism," a kind of fiction that systematically interweaves realism and fantasy, many of its distinctive narrative techniques appear elsewhere in Kroetsch's fiction. The indeterminacy of boundaries pervades his novels and seems to constitute a preoccupation, even an obsession, in all his work. The origins of this preoccupation may be found in Kroetsch's early life. He was born in Heisler, Alberta, and grew up on the family farm. As a child, he suffered from allergies that kept him from engaging in the work that farm boys normally performed. The society in which he lived possessed explicitly defined gender roles, the men working outside, the women inside, so he was not allowed to help the women of his family with their work about the house and in the kitchen. As a result, the family garden became his personal responsibility. This early experience with a garden — an in-between space (belonging to the house, but not in it; cultivated, but not farmed as a field would be) where the traditional spheres of male and female activity overlapped — seems to have made him both keenly aware of conventional gender roles and acutely conscious of all borderlands. Kroetsch recurrently observes borders that delimit the play of conventional female and male roles: interiors, food, and domestic rituals are usually female; exteriors, games, and narcissistic quests, male. His later experience as a student, university teacher, and writer in both Canada and the United States has given him a sense that, as he puts it, Canada is itself a "peculiar kind of border land," open to all manner of crossings. He underscores boundary situations and circumstances in many different ways, but he invariably returns to characteristic human dilemmas such as personal identity, social belonging, desire, and rejection. In *What the Crow Said*, the town of Big Indian is itself an indeterminate place, straddling the border between Alberta and Saskatchewan, isolated from the larger world yet influenced by it, ignorant of the world's technologies yet using them, at once primitive and contemporary, idiosyncratic and typical. However, many other kinds of indeterminacy — physical, social, and psychological — are evident in Kroetsch's other novels.

All of Kroetsch's novels, except his first and his most recent, concern Alberta at least in part. *The Man From the Creeks* (1998) is set in Alaska and Yukon during the Klondike Gold Rush in the late 1890s. His first novel, *But We Are Exiles* (1965), is set in the Northwest Territories and returns to his experience as a young man working on the Mackenzie River. It develops themes, such as exile, quest and metamorphic identity, that remain important in all of Kroetsch's subsequent writing. One of his most characteristic ideas, that human beings can consciously reshape and hence elect their personalities, already appears clearly in *But We Are Exiles*. In his second novel, *The Words of My Roaring* (1966), Kroetsch explores a moment in Alberta's history, the emergence of Social Credit. His narrator is an exuberant, loud-talking political opportunist — a Kroetschian embodiment of male energy who is consciously reshaping himself, finding in the possibilities of a new politics the opportunities for self-fashioning. Along with his two subsequent novels, *The Studhorse Man* (1969) and *Gone Indian* (1973), it forms what Kroetsch calls a "triptych," although the connections between the three novels are not narrative but rather those of "juxtaposition, repetition, contrast." *The Words of*

My Roaring (an allusion to the twenty-second Psalm) constitutes the first of Kroetsch's experiments with narrative voice, a fascination with one important element of narrative technique that also appears forcefully in *What the Crow Said*. The central character of *The Words of My Roaring* is the first of a line of male characters who are unashamedly narcissistic, energetic, ambitious, sensual, and "hellers" with women. They all represent Kroetsch's idea of the "Canadian voice," which, unlike its supremely confident American counterpart, always expresses "the ironic awareness of man's littleness," even in the unfolding of narcissistic ambition.

The Studhorse Man, for which Kroetsch received a Governor General's award in 1970, recreates the region of Alberta southwest of Edmonton (approximately equivalent to the domain of Kroetsch's childhood) towards the end of the Second World War. It was a time of great change, the mechanization of rural Alberta creating a pervasive revolution in life, and Kroetsch's metaphor for this transformation is the figure of a studhorse man fruitlessly looking for a mare with which to breed his stallion. *The Studhorse Man* shows Kroetsch to be a master of comic description and characterization. *What the Crow Said* contains a large number of comic situations in which an exuberant series of actions concludes with an ironic comment: for example, the account of the death of Joe Lightning, who falls from an eagle's claws into a toilet pit but survives the fall, "not a bone of his body broken," yet drowns when the churchgoers who witness Joe's fall decline to help him because they "had on their Sunday clothes." This comic method, narrative exaggeration (or exuberance) capped by an ironic comment, is clearly evident in *The Studhorse Man*. (Kroetsch has observed of his writing that he has a "sense of irony that threatens to destroy me.") Irony in the form of understatement and reversal permeates his characters' speech and the storytelling voices of his male narrators.

The third novel in Kroetsch's Alberta triptych, *Gone Indian*, explores a familiar region of in-between space, the Canadian/American cross-over land. The novel possesses two narrators, one a Canadian academic who has a university position in the United States, the other an American graduate student who comes to

Alberta; each is given a distinctive voice. The Americanized Canadian writes, but the Canadianized (more exactly, Aboriginalized) American narrates into a tape recorder. *Gone Indian* embodies a further experiment in narrative voice since Kroetsch not only doubles the voice (which he had already done in *The Studhorse Man* by putting the protagonist's story into the words of an incompetent biographer), but also contrasts the possibilities of written to oral narrative. The equivocal American voice (modified by its Canadian experience), filtered through and reshaped by the Canadian voice (which has fully accepted the configurations of American experience), is a typical Kroetschian situation along the boundaries of human possibility.

Badlands (1975), Kroetsch's fifth novel, concerns another moment in Alberta's history: the paleontological explorations of the Red Deer River valley in the first third of this century, which provided the fossil displays for many of the world's museums. The novel is still a further experiment in narrative voice. For the first time, Kroetsch creates a female voice, Anna, the repressed, middle-aged daughter of an Ontario paleontologist whose nearly forgotten field notes underlie the narrative. Kroetsch then doubles this voice by creating a second woman character, Anna Yellowbird, aboriginal and completely unrepressed, who acts as a muse to the first. Together, both women re-create the field notes of the first Anna's father, who has left a tantalizing, terse, and narratively undeveloped record of his 1916 Alberta expedition. Kroetsch's female narrator (with her female muse) re-invents her father's adventures with masterful irony. The male ambition, dreams of fame, tall tales (one of the men on the expedition recounts how he had copulated with Anna Yellowbird while inside the cone of a tornado), games and competitions, vulgar sexuality, and exaggerated male language are all seen from a unmistakably female perspective, mocked and debunked.

Kroetsch's novels after *What the Crow Said* — *Alibi* (1983), *The Puppeteer* (1992), and *The Man From the Creeks* (1998) — expand the range of his fictional worlds. *Alibi* begins in Banff and centres upon Calgary, but the action reaches into Europe (in particular Greece); in *The Puppeteer*, a loose sequel, the action shifts from

British Columbia to Greece. Considered within the context of the entire body of Kroetsch's fiction, however, what stands out from the two most recent novels is their interest in conceptual problems. Kroetsch has always been fascinated by narrative problems (a story's "truth," say, the number of its possible variants or the kind of "voice" it requires) and by the aporetic nature of play (what happens in a game? how can players believe in them so totally? what are a game's temporal limits? are the 151 days it takes to play schmier in *What the Crow Said* fabulous or wholly within the limits of ordinary possibility?), but *Alibi* and *The Puppeteer* foreground another kind of problem, more abstract and cerebral. They probe the concept of a collection, in particular that which takes the form of a museum. A Calgary millionaire (a recessive game-master in *Alibi*; the narrator in *The Puppeteer*) obsessively collects collections, whole collections that other collectors have already put together. Part of the appeal of collections for a writer such as Kroetsch lies in the arbitrariness of all human systems: anything can be collected in various ways; broken up into smaller collections; absorbed into larger ones, such as a museum. The concept of a collection suggests the shifting unreliability of all human attempts to confer identity upon the unsteady "reality" that exists beyond language. It is this arbitrariness and sheer fictionality of collections that make them such a powerful metaphor for fiction. In Kroetsch's two novels after *Badlands*, both highly self-conscious concerning their standing as fiction, collections represent the whole spectrum of problems associated with language, thought, and fiction. The motif of a collection captures, if only parabolically, the fissured, open, and endlessly metamorphic networks of language. The focus upon narrative in Kroetsch's earlier fiction becomes, without disappearing, a more cerebral romp among the problems of mind.

The Man From the Creeks, his 1998 elaboration of a famous Robert Service poem, turns away from the playful investigation of conceptual problems and towards Kroetsch's earlier fascination with narrative voice and the rhetorical strategies of storytelling. How small can a story be? Can a mere name add up to a character? What happens when one storyteller expands another's minimal narrative? *The Man From the Creeks* develops a few narrative hints in Service's poem, "The Shooting of Dan McGrew":

> Pitched on his head, and pumped full of lead,
>   Was Dangerous Dan McGrew,
> While the man from the creeks lay clutched to the
>   Breast of the lady that's known as Lou.

Kroetsch's narrator, as in the early novels a male with plenty of hindsight and mocking irony, is Lou's son. Now 114 years old and still living in Dawson City, Peek recounts how he and his mother made it over the Chilkoot Trail from Skagway in the company of a cooper from Iowa. Once they reach it, Dawson City turns out to be a typically in-between place, crowded with people from all over the world, all of whom have abandoned their homes, their previous habits and values, in the search for gold. In Kroetsch's novel, Dawson City is an indeterminate, constantly changing place characterized by individual self-fashioning and collective transvaluation. In other words, it is a vast archive of stories waiting to be told. The minimal story in Service's poem is fleshed out into a full-scale narrative body. Dan McGrew becomes a character with a history and habitual mannerisms; the "man from the creeks" is given a name, complex personality, and mind; Lou now possesses all the baggage that a human being normally carries into new experiences, including a son. Above all, Kroetsch's novel clarifies the uncertain and ambiguous ending of Service's poem. The novel ends as a good narrative should: with both a backwards look that places everyone exactly, drawing out the story's full implications, and a sudden, unpredictable ironic perspective.

What the Crow Said reflects aspects of all of Kroetsch's other novels while being, in many respects, the most distinctive of them all. Although it deals with a moment in Alberta history, the post-Second World War transition of rural Alberta into modern technology-based agriculture (and into the recognition that the rest of the world exists), it is an imprecise time, nearly as much so as its imprecise space and location. The people of Big Indian drive square, boxy cars (Vera Lang drives an Essex), but at one point a flight of F-104s screams across the valley. In the light of Kroetsch's other fiction, what stands out most sharply is his fascination with the ways in which stories are told.

In all of his novels, Kroetsch incorporates numerous forms of traditional oral storytelling, such as anecdotes, yarns, tall-tales, and jokes. The field notes that provide the starting point for *Badlands* are another paraliterary form of narrative in that, like the anecdote or the joke, they are essentially adumbrations, minimally conceived and expressed — just bare bones waiting for narrative flesh. Kroetsch delights in all narrative forms, but especially those that seem to wait in expectation of a more complete, more thorough-going development. Historically, one important facet of the novel as a genre has always been its capacity to absorb other, less developed ways of telling stories, incorporate them, fill them out, and transform them into literature. Any kind of writing — lists, letters, notes, technical documentation, journal entries, graffiti, even pictographs and hieroglyphics, whatever the imagination insists upon — can fit into a novel, fall into place, and become an integral aspect of the novel's discourse. Kroetsch is a master of this literary alchemy. His readers can encounter him returning, over and over, to the problems of telling stories, of suggesting the possibilities of story, and even of telling a story without telling it. (This development of minimal story elements into a fully realized narrative, most striking in *Badlands* and *The Man From the Creeks*, is also an aspect of Kroetsch's poetry. It is worth remembering his 1981 volume of poetry entitled *Field Notes*.)

However, the other side of Kroetsch's fascination with narrative lies in his careful experiments with narrative voice. Every story must be told, and the voice that tells must inevitably possess distinctive characteristics: an idiom, a vocabulary, turns of phrase, ways of stressing or ignoring its surrounding world. In each of his novels, beginning with *But We Are Exiles*, the narrative voice has been a central factor, perhaps often what the reader will most clearly remember, at once a vibrant experiment in narrative structure and a vigorous, unforgettable character.

From the first words of *What the Crow Said*, the reader knows that the novel's narrative voice will be unusual: "People, years later, blamed everything on the bees...." The voice speaking, inviting readers into a good story, is an actual character, although they will never meet him (or her) but only hear his voice. He knows the intimate details of life in Big Indian, he can imagine hidden desires and other motivations, and he is, like other Kroetsch characters, heavily ironic. Above all, he speaks collectively. He is the voice of the entire community over a period of twenty-five years. "People," he observes at a crucial moment many years after the opening incident, "before the day was over, would recall the afternoon, twenty-four years earlier, when the spring sunshine brought a swarm of bees to the district." He knows everything that matters, and his memory runs back and forth over everything that his happened since the springtime moment when the swarm of bees raped Vera Lang. Knowing, ironic, and collective, the novel's voice builds Big Indian for the reader, capturing its vivid local detail, its many fabulous events, the historical continuity, and the in-between nature of its collective experience.

> The roar was an animal roar. Some remembered it, after, as a bull sound, ferocious, out of the dark earth itself, the sound of the darkness itself. Some remembered the horses that drowned when Skandl's lighthouse broke through the ice, the lost and drowning team abandoned by all, trumpeting a perfection of despair. Some thought a pack of wolves was loosened on the town, purely and simply rabies mad, yelping and howling to a final feast.

"They" — "some" "people" — have told the story of Big Indian, and the narrator reports what has happened as versions of what has been said. This might seem like deliberate vagueness, a narrative refusal to make things clear. What it actually does is to summon the many different voices of the community, over a period of years, speculating, advancing hypotheses, telling quite different stories about the same event. The narrator's reiterated "some" evokes the experience, told and retold in different story-versions, of Big Indian itself.

Kroetsch's collective narrative voice in *What the Crow Said* is one reason the novel has sometimes been called "magical realist," aligning it with the body of Latin American literature that, with an explosive boom, invaded the consciousness of North American readers after the publication of the translation of Gabriel García Márquez's *One Hundred Years of Solitude* (1967). Magical realist fiction typically mixes the most ordinary incidents with the most fabulous, and it does so within a narrative voice that never shows astonishment, never expresses bafflement at even the most unusual occurrence, and does not seek either natural or supernatural explanations. In an interview in 1977, Kroetsch remarked of García Márquez, acknowledging the power of his writing, that he "nips at the heels of realism and makes the old cow dance." But there is more to magical realism than simply mixing realistic and fantastic incidents. Cuban novelist Alejo Carpentier once characterized the fictional blending of the real and the marvellous as the expression of primitive faith. The characters of fiction must possess the unquestioned faith in what happens, or seems to happen, that the unsophisticated inhabitants of certain primitive societies may evince. (The inhabitants of Kroetsch's Big Indian, although perhaps neither primitive nor unsophisticated, never question the reality of events, although Isador Heck, at one point in his fictional existence, does question whether the world itself exists, "speculating that if anything did in fact exist, there was no reason to believe it was visible." And *that* conjecture is anything but primitive.) Given Kroetsch's emphasis upon the importance of oral literature, it is easy enough to see that magical realism, eliciting the underlying structures of collective belief, could have attracted him.

On the other hand, scholars have often pointed out that South American magical realism is only a new version, with its local geographical and social variants, of traditional European fantasy. Anyone who has read Franz Kafka, *The Trial*, say, or *The Metamorphosis*, will remember that fiction in which characters simply accept, or possess faith in, what happens to them is hardly a South American invention. It might even be argued that to have read Homer is, always and already, to have read magical realism. Thus in reading *What the Crow Said*, it doesn't much matter whether the reader assumes that the author is experimenting with an innovative new form of fiction from South America or is calling upon the traditional resources of European literature. What does matter is that Kroetsch writes originally and uses all the vast potential of narrative to evoke rural Alberta and to reveal some of its hidden surprises — the nooks and enigmatic recesses of a consciousness that, before his fiction, had been only incompletely explored.

ROBERT KROETSCH

For Smaro and Megan and Laura.

People, years later, blamed everything on the bees;

it was the bees, they said, seducing Vera Lang, that started everything. How the town came to prosper, and then to decline, and how the road never got built, the highway that would have joined the town and the municipality to the world beyond, and how the sky itself, finally, took umbrage: it was all because one afternoon in April the swarming bees found Vera Lang asleep, there in a patch of wild flowers on the edge of the valley.

The coulees and the flats along the Bigknife River were too rough for wheat farming so the sod was never broken; the crocuses bloomed in spring as they had always bloomed, the buffalo beans cracked yellow, the violets and the buttercups and the shooting stars took their turn. Perhaps Vera had gone simply to pick a bouquet of crocuses, or to gaze down into the long, clay-shouldered trench of the valley, at the meandering river still locked in ice, at the town of Big Indian, its six grain elevators, its gravel streets, hardly a mile downstream, and yet so distant from the farm.

Why she took off her clothes, no one explained that either; nor why she lay down: perhaps it was the April wind, and the breaking clouds, and a girl's — a young woman's — simple desire, after a spring rain, to dream in the spring sun. But when she first stirred awake, out of her unexpected sleep, the bees were already arriving. Scouting for a nest, a new place to hive, the first bees had found the scent of her sun-warmed body. What her terror must have been at the soft caress of those touching bees, at the trickle of gold along her bare thighs; what ultimate desperation caught in her throat at the ferocious and innocent need of those homeless bees, at the feverish high hum, she never told. Locked into silence, she lay as transfixed as death, the bees hunching headlong into the first resistance of her blonde pubic hairs.

Vera's younger sisters, somewhere, all five of them, were searching, first in the barn where she might have gone to gather eggs. They hopped like the chickens themselves, pretending to cackle, straying their way up the straw-hid wooden steps. They looked in the back stall, where Vera had nursed and groomed a sick calf through the winter. They left the barn, shut off the windmill where it turned in the April wind, the watertank overflowing; they straggled across the muddy yard up to the tall, gaunt, wooden house.

While Vera, south of the house, south of the garden, sheltered from the wind by a poplar bluff on the valley's edge, watched the bees break cluster on a poplar branch. The broken cluster swarmed gray-brown and humming into the air, bloomed yellow-brown into the air; the bees, too, waiting; like a grotesque blossom they swayed above the suddenly naked branch, the great flower itself breathing, pulsing itself large, contracting, swelling again, as huge as a house that had bloomed into the air. Vera's whole life, ascended into the helpless air, giving a shadow to the pinched sky. The bees, without their queen, waiting.

Vera's five sisters, remembering their mother's urgent request, paraded in a straggling row up the three steps and across the porch, through the entry. They dawdled past the cream separator and the milk pails, through the room called a summer kitchen, though now it was the kitchen proper. They poked lazily through sun-warmed rooms where flies buzzed against the windowpanes. They went up the dark stairway. They snooped in their grandmother's trunk. They spilled out into the garden behind the house, the long garden reaching down from the slight rise to the shelterbelt at the garden's bottom, almost at the valley's edge. They peeked in at the outhouse, checked the three unpainted granaries that stood in a row near the barn, went to the machine shed and climbed up on a binder, sat and bounced in turn on the iron seat, then went to the pig barn, then wandered back to the corral where the bull should have been.

While their mother, Tiddy Lang, held the bull at bay with her shook skirt and apron. For the bull had got into the pasture north of the barn at a time when Martin Lang did not want his milk cows bred. Martin Lang, who was always in town when he was needed, always in the beer parlor in the Big Indian Hotel, doing anything but farming. And Tiddy must alone, as always, keep the farm in its thriving; a woman with six daughters when she needed one ambitious son, with an ordinary husband when she needed a paragon; she stood against the red bull, its savage pawing, its snorted breath.

While Vera closed her eyes to the whine, to the high, electric hum, of the bees' coming. Out of the wind that lolloped over the trees they took degree and angle; they took from returned scouts the final dance of direction. Their queen arose. The bees, streaming, shaped into a streamer of brown and gold, high in the sparkle of sun, began to drift toward the place where Vera waited. Without quite opening her eyes she knew they had touched down onto her arms, onto her belly, her legs. For how long she lay transfixed there was never a way to tell. Somewhere, long ago, the queen had been impregnated, her body never more to need that mating. Why the drones followed her, why they mistook a swarming into a new nest for a mating flight, was simply a mystery. Vera, the bees in her blonde hair now, touching onto her cheeks, could only lie still. She felt on her whole body the cloaking bees like a garment of black and gold, a living garment. The woman herself was still. The covering bees fell out of the sky, the first arrived, already, crawling down into the space between her slightly parted thighs.

The sisters had not found her, could not; and in their growing concern they pressed their grandmother, Old Lady Lang, into the search. She was in the cellar breaking the sprouts off last fall's potatoes. The weather, too warm too soon, had set them to sending up long, pale sprouts, out of the darkness of the bin. She hobbled up the cellar steps, into the sudden light and stood for a moment, blinking, clutching in the folds of her apron the special ball of sorrow that was hers. She had been there from the beginning, Old Lady Lang. Gertrude Lang, in her black dress, in her endless mourning not at any particular death but at the inevitable absence. "It's too sad," she would say, "I don't want to think about it." She crossed the yard, past the windmill, in through the front door of the big red barn and out the back. She saw her daughter, saw the bull. "Your cousin is in town," she said. "Put a chain on the ring," she said, pointing to the brass ring in the bull's nose.

Vera, alone at the edge of the valley, lifted her body against the pressing bees. Her not daring to resist became the excuse, the cause of her slow yielding. She lifted her hips against the pressing, her long pale legs spreading to the weight of the bees, the slow surging of the bees. Her body joining their urgency. The drones, bigger, slower, moving with a hot deliberation, seeking always the hiving queen. Vera herself, swarmed into a new being. Her body singing like a telephone wire. Her nipples swelling and throbbing to the kiss of wing and leg, her belly tightening to the push and rub of her myriad unthinking lovers. She was enveloped. Her eyelids wore each a bee. Her armpits opened to the nuzzling bees. They found the spaces between her fingers, between her toes. Her body was not hers now, it moved with the surge of grass in the wind, a field of green oats, a flowering of clover. Her moving crushed the blue-purple petals of the crocus bed, broke the hairy stalks, the blossoms, into the dizzying sweetness of her own desire. The hum of wings melded earth and sky into the thickness of her skin. She had no mind left for thinking, no fear, no dream, no memory. The bees had closed her mouth, her ears. The bees found the swollen lips between her thighs; she felt their intrusive weight and spread farther her legs.

Then she gave her cry.

Big Indian, at that hour, was quiet. The train came into town from the west three days a week, returned on alternate days. But the clanging of cream cans being unloaded had not yet begun. The drayman had rattled his team and wagon through the gravel streets and stopped beside the platform. The egg crates were stacked and ready for loading. The farmers were sitting quiet in the spring sun, in front of the hardware store, in front of the pool hall. Doors were propped open along Main Street, the businessmen inside waiting for shipments of parts for machinery, waiting for the farmers to stir alive before going home to supper and to chores. They had expected, all those waiting men, to hear the train whistle, for the CNR bridge, a mile below the town, was also a bridge for cars and wagons. No one had ever got around to building a road bridge to join the town to the north bank of the river. Planks laid beside the tracks on the one-lane railway bridge were sufficient. Every driver, even the engineer of a train, must announce his coming.

They had expected a steam locomotive's whistle, all those loafing and waiting men; they heard a sound that was almost human. Far distant to their ears and yet clear too. They could not describe it later, those same men, and yet there were surely as many of them, that day, in Big Indian, as there were drones in the swarm of bees. A coyote, one man said; but not at this time of day, another answered. Terrified and prolonged, but not a cry for help; despairing and ecstatic too. At first it was a cry of joy, a joy inhumanly exquisite; then it released a sorrow beyond all sorrow. They knew then, the men outside in the streets, the women in their houses, it was a human outcry, pain-filled and sweet, beautiful, wild, terrified. From up the valley, not from down. They knew, the women sitting over coffeecake and gossip before they started supper, they knew it was a woman's outcry, lament and song in one, even if they did not know its secret origins, its wail and hardihood of source. They guessed, the boys in school, dreaming away the last half hour before escape; they heard and looked to their teachers' faces, guessed they were confronting a mystery greater than any they were expected to or ever would learn. The old priest, alone in his rectory, poured himself a secret glass of wine.

She opened her thighs. Vera reached, gently, with careful, fero-cious hands, pulled wide her own thighs. The bees moved. It was love, it was pure love, her body beginning to move, again, unable to stop and yet no longer urgent, the hiving bees arriving home, the whole nectar of her world-old virgin body poured into their instinct to begin again. The men, below her, downriver in the valley, in the town: they heard the surrendered call. Years later, they would claim to have smelled the moment too: the crocus and cold earth smell, the smell of spring earth, breaking alive. Vera, moving, not able not to move, crushing the silken stems of the crocus bed, breaking the petals back from their pollen-yellow tongues. They heard the outcry of her painful joy, those men, the extremist coming; they heard, each of them, and they knew. Not knowing her name, or where she was, or what had touched her into that fierce and passionate and desperate ululation: they knew no man would satisfy her. Not one. No mortal man would satisfy her.

That was the year the snow didn't melt.

After those few hot days in April, the cold returned. Along the Bigknife River a thaw would set in for a day or two, yes, but then a cold snap would follow and with it would come more snow. Vera Lang, writing the district news for the *Big Indian Signal*, reported that the rabbits weren't quite losing their white coats. The horses weren't shedding. Twice in the course of six weeks she slipped into her column the irrelevant remark: men are a bunch of useless bastards. The wheatfields, she went on in each case, aren't quite workable…Not that people really complained; the snow became a handy explanation, an excuse, a useful provocation, even an absolute truth. When Vera announced that she was pregnant, her mother, seated at the end of the kitchen table nearest the stove, looked out over the heads of her six daughters, out through the south window, into the failing light of the June evening.

"It's snowing," Tiddy said.

She stood up from the table and went to the door. She took down her coat.

Liebhaber was playing pocket pool.

He was standing at the front window of the newspaper office, dreaming a woman for himself, idly watching the buzz of snowflakes, like myriad white bees, against the glass. That was the first time he remembered the future. A figure walked by, strode past or seemingly through the frost patterns of leaf and fern, hands pressed to bare ears, jacket open. And Liebhaber, then, remembered: Martin Lang was going to die during the night. He started to set the story, slightly in advance of the event; that too was simple enough. Time was something of a mystery to Liebhaber. Page one of the *Big Indian Signal* needed filling. He returned from the window to the composing room. He picked up the composing stick; he bent to the Hamilton drawers; he flicked the letter M into place: *Martin Lang, long-time resident of the Municipality of Bigknife, passed away unexpectedly…*

Unexpectedly? Was it fair to say unexpectedly? Something had gone awry in the district, since the afternoon of the bee swarm, back in April. But yes, Martin was the picture of good health: *on the night of June 11*. Martin, out there, walking in the blizzard: *He is survived by his wife, Theodora*...Liebhaber watched his fingers as if, abruptly, they were not his own. *He is survived...*

He went again to the front window. He found his overshoes in the cardboard box under the empty coat rack; he found his overcoat on a chair. One sentence about the widow and the page would be complete: *she, unable to guess her forthcoming sorrow...*

It wouldn't do. Liebhaber, at the window, put on his coat. He ought at least to say something, to tell someone. But he didn't go to the door. He returned to the composing room, to the Hamilton drawers, to case and font, ten point, eight point. The simplest matter, unexplainable: the innocence of a man who dressed in June clothing because it was June. He sat down on the stool and let his fingers try again: *and six daughters. Mr. Lang...*

Was a pioneer in the district...But he wasn't a pioneer, he'd married a cousin and farmed her farm...Mr. Lang was generous and public-spirited? Not with nine mouths to feed. He was sometimes tight-fisted. Except when in the beer parlor. Mr. Lang made a living. More or less. He showed up for meals on time. Usually. He went to bed tired. Or drunk. Or both. Or, for that matter, neither...Mr. Martin Lang of the Municipality of Bigknife was an ordinary man. He liked to go berry-picking. Yes, that was a curious thing about him. With a wife and six daughters and a mother-in-law in the house, he liked on a Sunday afternoon to take a pail and go by himself into the valley of the Bigknife River and pick saskatoons or chokecherries or even look for a raspberry patch. But that wouldn't do to finish a story...

Liebhaber had never missed a deadline in his life. He was beginning to sweat, inside his camel-pile overcoat. He started to look at his watch, then couldn't find it, inside all his clothing. He couldn't finish the story; he couldn't complete the page and add the quoins, check the footstick, the sidestick, lock up the form...

Liebhaber went out the door. He followed where Martin had walked. A team of horses, bowed, their blankets white with snow, waited in the empty lot beside the Big Indian Hotel: John Skandl the ice cutter's team. And a saddlehorse was there too, tied to the same telephone pole. Inside Martin Lang was seated at a table with John Skandl; Liebhaber joined them, raised his right hand to the slinger who slouched in front of the taps. He ordered six draft.

"Still coming down?" Martin asked.

Liebhaber indicated the snow on his overcoat. "Hell no." He felt a moment's irritation: a man, on the day of his demise, with the mercury falling, the roads drifting shut, should stay home with his family. He looked up at the wall clock but it was fast, set to bar time. Perhaps Martin was hanging around, delaying, because he'd come into town for the mail, for groceries, and wanted to take home with him the weekly newspaper. Liebhaber began to feel a weight, a burden on his shoulders. He unbuttoned his coat and tried to relax.

"Asshole of the universe," Martin said. "Even the gophers can't make a living."

"Funny damned break-up," Skandl said. "I can't cut ice because it's almost summer, and I can't sell ice because it's almost winter. This time it's belly-up for sure."

Liebhaber looked for words. He wanted to look with his fingers, not with his head; while Martin Lang went on talking like the district news that Vera sent in each week, that a dozen women sent in each week from a dozen corners of the municipality. Liebhaber, silent, consoled himself by letting the gossip click against his mind's pain: *Sunday supper guests at the Leo Weller home were Art and Lorna Van Slyke and Ken Cruickshank.* Yes, he liked best of all Vera Lang's submissions, the crabbed, tight, perfect handwriting on the page of scribbler paper that told him with impartial concern: *Also attending were Andy and Alice Wolbeck...*

Martin Lang ordered another round. Skandl found a few coins in his pocket, grandly signaled the slinger. Liebhaber let his mind try it: Mr. John Skandl, for the first time in history, voluntarily bought a beer. Liebhaber must each week set enough type to fill Wednesday's newspaper with words; the editor and publisher, Mr. Wills, in town for two days, leaving the heaped scrawls and scratches and guesses and advertisements in a basket, leaving his only instruction: "Make them fit, will you, Gus." That same Gus Liebhaber, his hands this one time telling him to snatch this one man out of his own story. Lang drunk now, gloriously drunk, happily drunk: and maybe that was the only story that mattered: the solitary man walking bare-headed through the fronds and leaves of frost on the front window, that blind man, able to believe that June was June: "One for the road, boys."

And Skandl, answering: "Colder than a witch's tit out there."

Liebhaber's fingers found a coin. He balanced the edge of the quarter over the nail of his right thumb, flicked; the coin spun high, straight up this time, straight up into the air, illuminating the sullen air with its reach and penetration, Liebhaber looking up to follow, to guess the zenith and the fall…

"The bees did it."

John Skandl, deftly, snatched the falling coin out of the air.

It was against the laws of the municipality for a woman to enter the beer parlor. Tiddy Lang was standing behind her husband, behind Liebhaber, facing Skandl. She lifted a scarf off her red hair and the snow fell on her husband's shoulders, fell on Liebhaber. "Someone must take a wife," she added, almost as an afterthought.

Years later, when he began to realize he could not remember something as simple as how he got to Big Indian, or how he learned the printer's trade, or where he came from, Liebhaber would still explain to himself: it was that remark that confounded him into buying a round for the house. Tiddy Lang, speaking in that awkward, pontificating, fatal, afterthought way: Someone must take a wife. The simple statement slammed through Liebhaber's mind like an exploding rock. It had all the excitement of theft about it, a vast and terrible conspiring to unhinge the world's illusions.

John Skandl, as if he'd heard nothing, slapped the caught coin onto his wrist. "Heads I win, tails you lose."

It was Skandl who dared to get her a chair. He stood up, huge, shaggy in his open sheepskin-lined coat; he pulled a chair from an empty table. Tiddy Lang had never in her life been in the Big Indian beer parlor. She shook her hair down over the fur collar of her coat.

"The bees did it," Tiddy insisted.

"Damn the bees," Martin said. "You can't come in here."

"Damn Vera and her daydreaming," Tiddy said.

Liebhaber began at that instant to understand Vera Lang. In the perfection of a long moment, Vera had mastered a disdain that reduced all men to strangers. One day in spring she had waited. Into the silence that followed, she sent outrageous messages; she slid them under Liebhaber's door on a Monday morning, dared him to print them on a Wednesday afternoon. *Mr. and Mrs. Bert Brausen are pleased to announce the engagement of their eldest daughter. The horses aren't shedding. Men are a bunch of useless bastards.*

Martin Lang laughed. "This weather. Freeze the nuts off an iron bridge."

All the world dumbfounded into an unending winter, and Martin sitting there, laughing over a table covered with glasses of beer; Liebhaber was appalled into a bitter outcry:

"By the blue-eyed Christ, you should go home."

"Why?"

"Because..."

"Because *why?* damnit. To work the summerfallow? To make hay? To plant green feed when there's snow on the ground? To poison gophers?"

Liebhaber, unable to argue. Confounded into dumbness by what he knew he knew. Tiddy Lang, not quite listening, aware that they were only men, and only talking. She brushed the snow from her red hair. Liebhaber saw her thick red hair, her redheaded woman's skin that was never quite tanned, for all the sun, all the wind; Liebhaber, in awe, in pain:

"The world is a double hernia."

"Might warm up in time for the grasshoppers to hatch," Martin said.

"A cracked pot. A boiled lemon. A scab and a carbuncle. A mole on a mole's ear. A mouthful of maggots."

Tiddy tried to say something. But now they were resisting, the three men; subtly they were not letting her exist in their secret place. They could not send her outside, into the storm. But they would not let her in either.

"You'll feel better in the morning," Martin said to Liebhaber. "If you don't catch cold."

"The world is a dog's tail and we chase it."

"Must be the green beer," Martin said.

Tiddy, again, tried to speak; the men, not letting her be there. Nothing was so important as her not being allowed to violate their secrecy. Liebhaber, too, in his outburst, excluded her from the misery of their loss and their terror and their loneliness. Liebhaber saw her hair, the perfect texture of her skin. She was immune to the sky, to the seasons. "I'm not going to die," he told her.

"You mean *work*, don't you?" Martin said.

Liebhaber was staring at Tiddy's long hands. He was almost a small man, his black hair almost hanging in his eyes, his eyes too large for his face, too dark, his black mustache too thick for his precise nose. "I'm not going to die. I won't." He was almost whispering. To Tiddy. Finally. He was speaking to Tiddy. "The world is a shedding snake. A skull. The scum and reek of a dead slough…"

"Green beer," Martin said. "It'll make you fart like a drayhorse."

Liebhaber emptied his own glass. He tried to steal one of Martin's in order to hasten the man along; he tried, attempted, strove with that one gesture to tell Martin somehow to avoid life for the evening, somehow to suspend himself for a night, for a turn of the world, out of time's way: "Damnit, Lang…"

A man came in from the blizzard. He seemed at first to carry with him an armful of the snow itself. Zike, the pressman, was an albino, his hair was almost yellow, almost as white as the snow he wore; a tall, lean man, sifted white now from head to foot. He hesitated, looking for a table in the shadowed room. He put down the papers; he knocked the snow from the top copy of the *Big Indian Signal*; he turned away; he slammed shut the door behind him as he departed.

Women went to bed easily with Zike. It didn't count, they said; he was an albino. It didn't count with Zike, who lived in the basement under the newspaper office, while Liebhaber lived in the flat above. It didn't count with Zike, his bed there close to the furnace, the crumbling cement walls hung with calendars, with every type and year of calendar he had ever printed, the basement divided into rooms by boxes of calendars that hadn't sold. He never tore the month of January off a calendar pad.

Tiddy, perhaps, thought he would make a husband for Vera. She buttoned her coat. She selected a coin from the pile of bills and change on the table in front of her husband. She put on her scarf. She stood up and went to the stack of newspapers and dropped a coin, picked up a newspaper and went to the door.

4

They were outside the beer parlor, the three men. They had somehow, leaning against the wind-driven snow, leaning against the darkness itself, found the horses. The black mare's front left hoof was on the toe of Liebhaber's left overshoe. He tried to pull himself up into the saddle. He tried again. He knocked his knee against the mare's leg, accidentally persuaded her to take one step. The wind whipped his breath away and he ducked his head against the thick mane. He groped for the saddle horn that he'd lost when the mare moved. He'd put the wrong foot in the stirrup; he hoisted himself toward the saddle and came face to face with Martin Lang.

Martin was sitting on the horse with his bare hands clapped to his bare ears.

"You're so goddamned drunk," Liebhaber shouted, "you'll fall off the goddamned horse."

"What horse?" Martin said.

Liebhaber's foot slipped from the stirrup; he fell backwards, into the snow. He lay in the snow. "See what I mean, John?" He was shouting. "He's pissed right out of his skull. I got to take the dumb bugger home."

John Skandl let go of the halter rope. He reached and with one continuing motion lifted Martin over the cantle, placed him behind the saddle seat. He reached down to where Liebhaber was wrestling with the snow, wrapped an arm around Liebhaber's waist, heaved him flailing into the seat from which he'd removed Martin.

"You know which end is the head?"

Both men, shouting against the wind.

"I know a horse's ass when I see one."

Skandl tied the halter rope with a clove hitch onto the leather-covered horn. He whistled a command and the black mare started, turned her rump to the force of the blizzard. Liebhaber, in the monstrous gait of the mare's impatience, thrashed the dark with his arms, stiffened his legs and in the process discovered the stirrups; he found in the teetering night his precarious balance.

"East end of a horse going west."

Not shouting now, removed from the earth by his sudden ascent onto the mare's back, he groped for the reins; he pushed at the stiff reins, the mare beginning to drift with the blizzard, carrying her two riders away from the snow-filled shadow of the hotel. Martin Lang, leaning close behind Liebhaber, believing in June; they'd have to hurry. Liebhaber tried to kick his heels into the mare's belly.

And yet they were almost comfortable, the wind at their backs, moving down the dark, deserted street. It would take them east and out of town, towards the railway bridge with planks laid beside the rails. They must cross over on the bridge and double back, on the north side of the river. And they must watch for Tiddy. Tiddy in a huff. Liebhaber, watching: the hardware store that wasn't quite where it should have been, its dark windows full of rakes and hoes and garden seeds, unsold because spring had never come; the Chinaman's café, the wind swinging the one small light over the promise of a door; the Elks' Community Hall; the square, wooden, two-storey building that was the print shop and the office of the *Big Indian Signal*, and Zike's home, and his home too, Liebhaber's. The frosted front window was dark. He tried, again, to kick his heels into the mare's belly. They passed the last caragana hedge surrounding the last house, the last and final street lamp, the myriad snowflakes eating its light...

The grain elevators weren't there. The string of elevators, slope-shouldered, red; they weren't visible along the railway tracks that weren't visible either. Liebhaber sawed at the horse's reins. He might have turned back, had he known how. Perhaps he thought he had turned back when he felt the wind. He faced into the wind. Liebhaber couldn't see. The snow rattled on his stiffening cheeks. The hard, broken snowflakes pecked at his eyes. He was already turning back, he believed he was turning back, when the muffled squeak of hoofs on the snow-buried gravel road became, abruptly, a hollow drumming.

They were onto the bridge. They were not so much onto the bridge as out into the air itself, into the blizzard. They were out on the long, timber bridge. Liebhaber, for the first time, felt the embrace. He heard his own voice, "If Skandl had brought us…"

"If the dog hadn't stopped to shit" — Martin wrapped his arms tight around Liebhaber, hugged him; he shouted now, against the head-on force of the blizzard — "it would have caught the rabbit."

Martin was burying his face out of the way, against Liebhaber's back. Liebhaber found in a pocket of his camel-pile coat a toque. He pulled the toque down over his hair, over the snow in his hair. Martin's arms got in the way. Liebhaber, putting on the toque, let go of the reins. The bridge was a tunnel of black timbers that reached forward, into the lighter dark of the night and the blown snow. If the dog hadn't stopped…

He caught the saddle horn with both gloved hands, his fingers not quite working. Liebhaber, his feet held up by the stirrups, out of the rising flood. But they weren't on the bridge. The small poplars were stiff, their branches cutting at his face. They'd ridden into a ditch. Or onto a slough, the frozen slough ringed with willows, ringed with poplars. Liebhaber let go of the reins; the mare turned. He cupped his hands between his spread legs, between his body and the saddle. Perhaps he sat there for a long time before he realized the horse wasn't moving. He remembered the bridge. He remembered a barbed wire gate, a row of fencepost tops, motionless and upright in the swirling snow. They were out of the valley, up onto the plain. The two riders. Perhaps they'd missed the farm. Perhaps they sat there a long time, in the night, on the shapeless plain, not moving; it was only the world that moved.

Stiff arms all around him waved to the wind. The mare wasn't moving. Liebhaber tried to kick her into motion. He could not move his legs. There was enough light so he could see his useless knees. He was surrounded by a standing grove of underwear and sheets, of pillowcases and nightgowns and pajamas.

Martin had seized him from behind. Martin had surprised him, had raised his right arm across Liebhaber's chest, had tightened his left arm around Liebhaber's belly. Liebhaber, pawing the darkness with his frozen eyes: the forms, on their wires, stiffly swayed and heaved together. Snow fell, whirled down onto and around the frozen forms. Liebhaber eased his neck away from Martin's raised hand, pressed against the head behind his own. He tried to turn his face, tried to find the face that was close against his neck.

The two arms that held him did not relax. Liebhaber pushed his weight forward against the unrelenting arms, leaned back again, then tilted away from the kiss on his cheek. The hard, stiff kiss, on his brittle cheek, panicked him into motion. The mare stirred. The two men began to tilt sideways, slipping. Liebhaber let go of his crotch, groped for the saddle horn. "I saved you." He spoke again, "No. I saved you. God damn."

The mare, as quickly as she had started, stopped. Liebhaber saw it now: the gang plow, the two-bottom plow almost buried in the snow, the mare's front left leg stopped by an iron wheel. He reached to protect himself from the levers of the plow, found he had no free hands, no arms that were merely his with which to do the reaching. He caught the saddle horn again, held on, the stiff figure of Martin Lang, riding his back; Liebhaber, ridden down by the figure of Martin Lang, letting himself go, fighting and letting go too, stranded between the sky and the earth; he would never give in, never, he remembered that, plummeting. He fell back into Martin's arms. He felt the embrace loosen. Or, no: the indifference released him: he could not believe they had struggled. He lay, as if dropped, in the snow. He lay on his back in the snow.

Martin Lang, above him, was seated on the plow. One hand was raised above the other, both were raised out in front of the motionless figure. The three buttons of Martin's tweed jacket were unbuttoned. His hair moved; only his hair moved.

The frozen brassieres and bloomers swung gently on the invisible wires. Liebhaber could not get his legs under his body. He lay on his back, consoled; the tumbled and whirling flakes fell onto his face, onto his mouth and eyes, closed him against the inviting world; the flowering snow grew over his hands. He heard the bees; the bees, distant. He forced himself to turn; he turned onto his belly, turned again onto his back. Somewhere beneath the snow's surface, his legs would not work. He rolled in the snow, forced himself to roll, the bees coming down from the frozen bloomers, from the shoulders of a blouse. He would roll to the wind-cleared road where he might speed along like a rolled log; yes, he would, must, roll out across the prairies, find a clump of willows where he might briefly hide; then he would roll again, finding a strawpile, a haystack, a sleeping cow, a coyote's den. He believed he was rolling. Against all the rise and fall that constituted existence, he had found a solution. He believed he was rolling when he opened his eyes, when he saw Tiddy Lang.

Tiddy was not affronted by miracles. She'd heard the noise on the porch and had gone to the kitchen door and opened it. Somehow she lifted the frozen man, carried him by herself through the kitchen, through the dining room, into the bedroom beyond. Instead of going to the foot of the stairs, she returned to her reading of the front page of the *Big Indian Signal*. She studied again the blank space, the absence of words, at the bottom of the right-hand column. She read the space for a long time before she folded the paper, then laid it carefully at the base of the coal oil lamp, in the middle of the flowered oilcloth that covered her kitchen table.

Tiddy went to the wooden sink. She emptied the blue graniteware basin into the slop pail. She pulled the towel on its roller until she found a dry spot; she rubbed at her hands. Carrying the basin, she stepped out through the kitchen door. She returned with the basin heaped with snow.

The wind-packed snow broke, fell powder-like over Liebhaber's face. Tiddy massaged. She worked the snow against his ice-white cheeks. Liebhaber was whimpering now, crying softly. Liebhaber, crying. The million red hot needles were driven into his frost-scalded ears, into his frozen and thawing hands, his stubbed toes, his iron heels. Tiddy tugged off his gloves, worked the snow against the backs of his hands, against and between his stiff fingers. She undid his three-buckle overshoes and pulled them off; she brushed the snow from his shoes and untied them, removed his shoes, his socks.

The room was filled with Liebhaber's breathing. He could hardly gasp the hot air into his frost-strangled lungs. Tiddy unbuttoned his collar. She eased him out of his camel-pile coat. She stripped off his toque, his sweater and shirt, his undershirt too. She rubbed his bare arms, his chest, with snow. She massaged him with snow. Liebhaber went on gasping, clutching now at the pain between his thighs.

Tiddy, again, touched the flaked and held snow to his cheeks. She caressed his forehead. She touched the thickness of his eyebrows, the black of his mustache. She touched more snow to his sharp, muscled shoulders. She rubbed more snow into the hair of his chest, she rubbed his belly and the muscles tightened under her hands.

Only after a long time, after everything else had failed, did she unbuckle his belt. Liebhaber had come to the end of his endurance. He writhed and flapped on the bed. He gasped, his hands clutched between his thighs, his voice a guttural squawk of despair. Tiddy, at last, stripped off his trousers and underwear. She slapped, firmly, his bareness, trying to start him out of his pain.

Years later, Liebhaber would insist it was somewhere in that night that his memory of the past began to fail. Everything was erased, blanked into nothing by snow. The story of Martin Lang's common folly and desperate fate he took only as hearsay. He was naked, there in Martin Lang's bed. Tiddy capped his nakedness with snow. That she warmed him in her arms, that Liebhaber saw her smile, was only rank rumor. She, with her long, certain fingers, scooped snow from the blue enamelware basin; she sprinkled it down onto Liebhaber's private parts. What he remembered, if he remembered anything, was the bee-like swarming of the flakes of snow, out of her hand, down onto his parted legs.

5

Vera Lang went for help.

Not by the road that led to the bridge on the far side of Big Indian; rather, she walked straight down into the valley from the spot where she had first encountered the bees. Vera lived more outside than she did indoors, nowadays, in her search for places where she might, come spring, locate her first bee yard. She walked onto the frozen river. She found the granary, out on the ice, in which John Skandl lived.

Skandl's Mansion, they called it in the Big Indian beer parlor, because it was less even than a shack, hardly a hovel. It was an old, unpainted granary, with a window cut into one wall, a hole poked in the roof for the tin chimney that stood straight up from the barrel stove. Vera knocked at the shiplap door. Perhaps she was cold, in the tearing wind, and lifted the latch before she heard an answer.

John Skandl, in his long gray woolen underwear, his bent knees braced against the low sill of the window, was relieving himself. He had drunk too much beer. When the door opened, when the gusting wind wet him in his own urine, he could not stop, he could not turn away.

"He's sitting on the plow," Vera said.

Skandl, his knees slightly bent, his belly against the reflection of itself in the slightly raised window, went on pissing, his bladder as if forever replenished, piped and bolted and sealed into an everlasting source.

"He's plowing the snow," Vera said. She glanced from the smoking lantern, from the open tin of sardines on the homemade table, to the dirty blankets on the cot. She noted, in the far corner of the small room, by the cot, on the chunks of coal and in the coal dust, in the frost that outlined the boards of the floor, his ragged trousers.

"Mother sent me." Vera said. Vera Lang, polished as bright as stone, explaining that nothing else, ever, would have delivered her to this male indecorum, this pigsty of filth and stink. Vera, not yet come to the purpose of her visit. "I just now walked over from the other side."

"What?"

"He's plowing the snow," Vera said.

"*What?*" Skandl shouted.

"Martin," Vera said. She was beyond mere human sorrow. She was imperious, disdainful; she did not so much look at Skandl as not bother not to look. "Now."

Skandl was almost shouting. He gave himself a flick. "You crossed over. On the *ice?*"

The honeycombed ice of spring was useless to the railways. But Vera had crossed the river where there should have been open water, a black rectangular gap. He pulled himself, with a quick yet stately motion of his buttocks, back inside his underwear. He brushed where a trickle of urine ran icy cold down his leg.

6

skandl, stealing up behind the corpse.

In that journey of three dozen yards, or on the drive out from town, or even while he awakened the two men from his cutting gang and harnessed the team, he realized that the courting of Tiddy Lang had begun. A widow with a section of land to farm, with cattle out in the snow, with hogs in the barn, needed a husband. And he was no longer loser to the sun. The ice was forming, thickening now in a June freeze.

Martin Lang and his plow were motionless, the pale earth itself moving; in the black sky the moon, huge and bitter. It was the scene that Tiddy would never let her suitors forget. She, going to her bedroom window, to lift it open, to pull a blind, to adjust a curtain, would remember her husband, would see him, his left hand seeming to hold the reins of invisible horses, his right hand raised to crack a whip, his hair flowing. Martin Lang, plowing the snow.

Skandl was hardly a foot from the plow seat when he slapped both arms around Martin's waist.

The frozen corpse was locked to the plow.

The four-horse team came through the snow, broke a trail, out of the darkness, to Skandl's side. The outthrust legs of the corpse were caught in rods and levers. Martin Lang must be loaded into the sleigh, hauled into town to the furniture store where the dealer in furniture was undertaker too.

Bill Morgan, wiping at the frosted socket of his missing left eye, stopped the team: "We could wait until morning."

Skandl let go his embrace. He kicked the snow away from the iron wheels of the plow. "Get me a hammer."

Alphonse Martz stayed close to Morgan, huddled near him in the sleigh: "What did he say?"

Morgan shook his head.

"I'm deaf in one ear," Martz said, "and I can't hear out the other."

Bill Morgan jumped from the sleigh box. He stumbled stiffly on his cold legs and hit a clothesline. Groping then, he was busy; he broke the clothespins free from a towel, from a dress, from a suit of underwear. He took into his arms the stiff, frozen garments, piled them on his left arm like sticks of firewood, turned and hastened toward the house. Something moved in a bedroom window. That was all they noticed. They had not moved an inch, either of the waiting men, by the time Morgan returned. Morgan, pushing the handle of the hammer toward Skandl. Moving in recoil at the soft words, "Thank you"; dumbfounded by his own, "You're welcome." And before he could close his mouth against the cold he heard the first crack of the steel head of the hammer on frozen bone.

Skandl did not strike the levers or the rods. He struck a caught leg. But he had not swung hard enough. "Widow," he said. Aloud. Unaccountably. And then he struck again. The hammer cracked down. "Liebhaber," Skandl said. He smashed again, with the hammer.

Martin Lang was free of the plow. The three men, getting in each other's way, lifted the body from the iron seat, avoided the swinging motion of the legs, carried the corpse through the snow. They tried to slide it in at the open end of the sleigh box, and still the legs dangled. They pushed the corpse in at the back of the box, in under the heaped straw they'd used to keep Vera warm on the drive out from town. They did not cradle the corpse on the straw. They hid it from themselves, so they might not see or remember the raised arms, the legs that found their own directions inside the stiff pantlegs.

Skandl was in the sleigh, freeing the reins from the peg on the front of the box. He wondered for a moment if Vera Lang had actually crossed where he'd cut the ice from the river; he wondered if new ice was forming, perfect ice, that he could cut and sell by the carload.

He would not go back by the road. He would drive where Vera had walked, straight down into the valley, across the frozen river and into town. He must see the new ice with his own eyes, touch it. He was to be a rich man, and he deserved those simple pleasures.

Skandl swung the team across the garden, straight towards the valley's edge. The heads of the three men standing in the sleigh were above the drifting snow. Snow stretched the landscape into streamers of silver wire, under the pure light of the moon. The two hired men jumped from the sleigh. They knocked the staples out of a row of willow posts; they held down the three strands of barbed wire while the team and sleigh went across, then jumped onto the passing sleigh. The team plummeted down into the deep coulee. The drifting snow swept over the four horses, over the staring men.

Somewhere in that dawn, Skandl hit on the need for a beacon, a fixed point in the endless winter. He did not at first plan a lighthouse at all; that ambition came later. The three men hit a snowdrift that no team could go through or over. They circled. They took down more fences. They found the river; they found a rapids where the water was open and had to fight their way up a steep clay bank through drifts and bush. The valley was an opening in the earth; the snow itself, swept off miles of open prairie, dumped into the valley, seemed surprised at the bottomless fall.

He was explaining the need for a beacon, a simple marker on the endless reach of endless snow, a pinpoint, a light, a tower, when they drove in under the railway bridge. Morgan, with his one eye, happened to recognize the bridge overhead. They had passed the town, somehow, the three men. They turned.

Mr. Aardt, the undertaker, pressing his hernia with one hand, holding a rug over his shoulders with the other, came to the door of the furniture store. He hadn't been able to get home through the blizzard and had slept all night in a pile of rugs. John Skandl could not understand why Aardt was irritated at being awakened. He stepped towards the back of the sleigh. He reached into the load of straw as if to explain not only with the words he mumbled, but with flesh and blood too. He felt, cautiously, down into the straw. He felt his way down, then pushed at the snow-drifted straw. He laughed out loud, as if amused at his own fumbling, his own temporary confusion. He managed a grin for Aardt. After all, he was tired; he'd spent himself and his men. He gestured forward to the horses, each of them slumped, each with its head slumped forward and down, a hind leg cocked. Then, frantically, he kicked his way into the straw and snow, kicked both out the open end of the sleigh.

Skandl shouting: "Liebhaber did this to me."

"What?" Aardt, startled. Pressing his hernia as he spoke.

"Liebhaber. The sonofabitch. With his goddamned good intentions."

Then Aardt, lifting the rug closer around his bald head, stepped to the rear of the sleigh, saw too the absence, the gaping box, empty. The straw, kicked in Skandl's fury, spinning away in the empty air. The box of the sleigh, bare to the polished boards.

"You've gone and lost him."

Aardt, almost pouting, watching Skandl's flailing hands, his feet in the empty sleigh box still kicking.

7

On the evening of that same day the residents of Big Indian heard for the first time the far howling of the wolves. With the failure of winter to end, packs of timber wolves were moving out of the northern forest. The Municipality of Bigknife lay ambiguously on the border between the provinces of Alberta and Saskatchewan; no one, due to a surveyor's error, had ever been able to locate conclusively where the boundaries were supposed to be. The south end of the municipality, beyond the poplar bluffs and the fields of grain, faded into bald prairie and a Hutterite colony; the north end vanished into bush country and an Indian reserve. A trapper on the reserve claimed to have seen wolf tracks; a rancher, north of the Bigknife River, which divided the municipality into two equal halves, claimed to have lost a sick sheep to wolves. But no one in the town, up to that evening, had taken the rumors seriously. The thrilling call, out of the silence that followed the storm, created a sense of urgency; on the following morning, twenty men and boys went out to walk and ride through the stillness and the snowdrifts. They were looking for Martin Lang, they said. They walked out into the blinding sunshine, studied, warily, the mystery of snow-molded hollows and mounds. They carried rifles.

Death was loose in the Municipality of Bigknife. Everyone knew that, and no one gave better evidence than Gus Liebhaber. He lay in the Lang house, in Martin Lang's own bed, his ears wearing huge blisters, his face peeling down to flesh, the skin raised clear of his feet by pockets of water, his lungs seared, his fever raging, his body lost in its own swelling. He lay in that temptation to die, his fingers too sore to be flexed, his mind not quite his own.

He was incontinent: he pissed the bed every few hours, shit himself once or twice a day. The daughters of the Lang house turned all the pain of their loss into a concern for the suffering figure in their mother's bed. Tiddy took to putting diapers on the man. She rubbed his frost-burned skin with baby oil, dusted his behind with baby powder. Some nights she slept in the same bed; she held Liebhaber in her arms to soothe his muttering; lovingly, she caressed him down into sleep.

Only Vera refused to enter the downstairs bedroom. In the cold splendor of her isolation, arrogantly pregnant, concentrating on her new books on bees, she prepared for the season of honey that she was certain must come. She mocked the concern of the others. "Let him sleep," she would tell her sisters. "He's like a snake, shedding his skin." "Mr. Skandl has arrived again," she would tell her mother — Tiddy rubbing salve onto Liebhaber's feet, massaging his stiff knees — when Skandl's team and sleigh came jingling to the kitchen door.

Only Skandl was too busy to venture out into the snow-drifted coulees. The searchers came back with stories of dead calves and yearlings, alone as glacial boulders on the river flats. They found three horses frozen to death, still standing in the fenced corner of an open pasture. Dead deer seemed to have leapt into a heap in a snow-filled draw.

Skandl, from dawn to darkness, supervised the cutting and hauling of ice. Only in the late evening had he time to visit Tiddy. Old Lady Lang would try to outlast him, propped up by a cup of coffee at the kitchen table, dealing herself a hand of solitaire. One or two at a time the daughters retreated up the stairs to bed; Cathy first, complaining at being treated like the child she was; then Rita and Gladys, silent and dignified and afraid; then Anna Marie, putting away her comb, sullen; then Rose, already moving her lips in her night prayers; then Vera, putting a last and careful period to the district news that now would be set, without Liebhaber's editing, by Zike, the pressman. Then, and finally, Old Lady Lang would muse over her spread cards, staring at the ace of spades, the queen of hearts: "It's too sad. I don't want to think about it." She would slip the deck of cards into a pocket of her black dress. Her soft footsteps found the creaking stairs, faded into their own silence.

"The bastard is a fake."

Skandl, turning fiercely from where he watched the doorway to the dining room, reaching past the coal oil lamp, across the table, to touch the back of Tiddy's hand. He repeated what he'd said the night before, and the night before that, and the week before. And maybe the month before that too. He was losing track. Everyone was losing track of time.

"He's healthier than I am, even if his mind is darker than the inside of a cow. Let me haul the sonofabitch home to his ink."

Tiddy removed her hand from his, stood up from the table. She went to the stove and lifted a lid with the poker. She poked at the coals. She closed the stove and picked up the coffeepot.

"He's healing. He's healing, slowly."

"He always looked like death warmed over."

Tiddy bent toward Skandl's empty cup. She glanced away from the relentless blue of his eyes.

"I find him handsome."

"He's ugly as a mud fence."

Gently, gently reaching, Tiddy touched Skandl's huge hand where it opened around the coffee cup. She took his hand in her own, raised it to her face. Her face was almost flushed; her redheaded woman's skin. She liked the smell of horses. Skandl's hands, smelling of horses.

"It's snowing," she said.

It was August first. The house was quiet as a tomb, for no birds had come to that summer. The upstairs was quiet, Old Lady Lang not yet snoring. Liebhaber had remained insane, totally out of his mind, and only when he heard Tiddy speak that sentence, or when she repeated it, did he have a moment of lucidity.

"It's snowing," she said.

Tiddy, holding Skandl's hand, the smell of horses, to her face, to her mouth...

It was that single sentence, spoken from the kitchen, that accounted for the four minutes of coherence that Liebhaber was to experience during his stay in Tiddy Lang's house.

"He's useless as the tits on a boar," Skandl said. The mention of snow excited Skandl; he failed to remember that the sky was clear. "He's broke flatter than piss on a plate. He's a nutless wonder."

Liebhaber, hearing his rival speak in the kitchen, tried to sit up in bed. He was totally coherent and able to remember. In sweet, black jealousy he remembered that Tiddy had somewhere in the incoherent nights lifted his blankets and sheet, had let herself into bed beside him. Into the old and habitual darkness she had come, after the supreme clarity of Skandl's ice. Liebhaber, in love, remembered his sore hands healing onto Tiddy's body, remembered finding the full of her breasts to warm his cold mouth, the softness of her thighs to ease the itch of his frost-blackened skin.

She had hauled him into need, Tiddy, searching for the missing body there in her own bed, while the searchers prowled the world. Liebhaber definitely remembered.

"It's snowing," Tiddy repeated. A long resignation, a quickened intensity, entered her voice.

"I'm building a beacon," Skandl replied. "A kind of lighthouse-looking thing." His voice softened. "Maybe you can catch a glimpse of it from here..."

And Liebhaber, in bed, listening, heard the silence that followed. It was too long a silence, too long. It was that that got him out of bed; not the speech, but the silence. He struggled up onto the edge of the old bed, the walnut-colored steel bedstead; he stood up onto wobbly legs. He found the strange garment draped around his buttocks. When it slipped loose from his hips he let it fall to the floor. He took one step, another; because he must see for himself, either the snow or the beacon. He could not see both, he knew that. Liebhaber, at the window. He chewed a corner of his mustache. He thought at first it was Martin Lang he saw, seated on the plow, beyond the clothesline, in the dark night, plowing the snow.

A wolf moved, two wolves; perhaps in the desperation born of their hunger, they'd smelled out Skandl's team, tethered on the far side of the house; the two wolves nuzzling in closer, moving in the shadows beyond the plow.

Liebhaber turned from the window. He was master of his faculties for a total of four minutes. He limped, he hopped, growing stronger with each step, his heart racing, his head totally alive to the terror and relief and then the desire that swept into his loins; he found the bedroom door; he groped his way around the dining room table, toward the far light.

The kitchen went dark.

The kitchen was pitch black. Liebhaber, groping, found Tiddy. As if she had only then leaned across the table, had lifted a hand to the top of the globe, had blown out the lamp. His groping hands reached under her stooped body. He found the nipples of her breasts.

She was as naked as he. He was not surprised. It was only as it had always been, in her bed, and when the question of who was father was argued, later, in the Big Indian beer parlor, Liebhaber was willing, each time, to fight to death.

When, years later, any drunk or fool or hero had Dutch courage enough to suggest it was big John Skandl who sired the strange child, he had in the instant of his speaking to deal with Liebhaber's unaccountable wrath: the wrath of a man who could be aroused to fighting by nothing else on the face of the earth but who, in that one matter of ultimate truth, would take on a man twice his size, would take on two opponents, three. Liebhaber, with only love as his weapon. In the four minutes of his sanity and coherence he touched his left hand to the warmth at the back of Tiddy's thighs, held in his right hand the falling weight of her full right breast. Why she was naked, he never asked. He found with his healed mouth the round and invisible fullness of her buttocks, his fingers stroking the first softness of the small hairs at her body's openings, the quick of his tongue licking her first motion. The heat on his mouth, the smoke on his tongue.

"It's snowing," she repeated. Yes, she was crying, and his hands pulled her close. In the dark, she was crying, whether from joy or sadness he never knew; the strokes of his body sounded, first, like waves on a shore, then like the breaking of sticks to build a fire. Liebhaber, his body ferociously wise, listened. Perhaps he too, for that short while, dreamed the lighthouse. As all the men would dream it in that snow-buried town. A center. A beacon. A guide. A warning sign. On the ice on the river, a high flame in the closing night. Liebhaber dared to speak. He whispered: "I love you." Gently, he whispered. His voice was hardly as loud as a kiss, as a folding wing…

And when the fist struck him, he was already spent; he was collapsing. The arms caught him from behind.

When he awoke he could see the stars. He was lying in the straw in the back of Skandl's sleigh. He tried to turn over. He listened. He could hear, under the far silence of the stars, the steady rhyme of the bells and harness on the necks of the trotting horses.

Skandl was talking to the horses. "Giddyup," he said. "Easy, boys," he said.

Liebhaber, wide-awake, let his hands find their way through the straw. The blow of the fist had gashed his temple. He was wearing, over a bandage, his toque. He was wearing his camel-pile coat. He couldn't quite remember. He lay still for a long time, watching the stars. He tried to turn over and couldn't. Then he saw, recognized, the figure of the bull. It was a bull, head down, wearing the stars as ornaments; the bull in the sky was coming straight at him. He closed his eyes and waited.

8

The courting of Tiddy Lang took on a ferocity that was a match for the weather itself, for the very wolves that inhabited the weather. On the Sunday following Liebhaber's departure, the Lang yard was full of square-bodied cars that had just that morning been cleaned of cigarette butts and empty beer bottles, full of horses that looked as new curried as dawn. The women of the house could hardly find room to go about outside, doing the day's chores. Rose, complaining bitterly all the while, went across the crowded yard in late afternoon, lifted the ice-sheathed axe in her mittened hands and chopped a hole in the ice in the watertank. Shivering by the windmill while the cows and horses drank, trying to amuse herself, she accidentally stuck her tongue to an iron rung of the ladder that went up the windmill's side. She hollered and groaned for help until the heat of her breath freed her torn skin. Not one of the visiting men could spare a moment away from Tiddy.

They came from all over the municipality, the suitors. Some of the widowers, when they arrived, were half drunk on chokecherry wine or potato champagne. Some of the bachelors arrived with frail excuses: they must report that a cow of Tiddy's had gone through a fence, a horse might be down in a strawpile. But they arrived, inevitably, found space in the yard for still another car or truck, still another team of horses. A man came all the way from the south of the municipality on a lug-wheeled John Deere tractor, the two-cylinder machine popping its way along the frozen horizon. The four members of a curling rink arrived in a closed-in cutter; they carried their brooms with them into the house. Two coalminers from up the river valley delivered a load of coal in the back of their jitney. A fish peddler arrived from the edge of a lake at the northern edge of the municipality, a ton of frozen whitefish, stiff and cold eyed, in the box of his sleigh. A Rawleigh man showed up with his wares and nearly sneezed to death while bragging about the freshness of his pepper. No one would bother to so much as slap his back.

Vera, watching over the crowded kitchen and dinning room and parlor, was able to address more than half the men by their first names because of her attempts to locate sites for bee yards, in preparation for the inevitable arrival of spring. She greeted, all the while barely concealing her disdain, eleven farmers, a moonshiner and a chicken thief.

Tiddy, that Sunday, invited the suitors to stay for supper. The next Sunday, however, she asked her mother to send each and every one of them away; and then she sat at the window of her bedroom alone, no light in the room; and through the window she saw him again, Martin Lang, out in the moonlit night, plowing the snow.

If they had found the corpse, the few men who went on seeking it, then something might have changed. The digging of a grave, attendance at a wake, the ceremony of burial, any one of those events might have made things normal again. The bees were to blame. The suitors, puzzled by Tiddy's shifting moods, her explosions of gaiety, her long silences, her moments of song, her unexpected touching of a forearm, a bare neck — the confused suitors, leaving her yard, looked up into the dark August sky expecting a swarm of bees to pursue them across the fields of dirty snow. They glanced back at the disappearing house, at the light in an upstairs window; they imagined Vera Lang, cold, aloof, polished as bright as stone, bending over her books on bees. They hated Vera. Only Liebhaber, on a weekday night in the Big Indian beer parlor, said nothing against her. He concentrated on hating Skandl.

John Skandl had conceived the notion that he would destroy all his rivals — Liebhaber first — by constructing, out of blocks of perfect ice, a lighthouse.

Swamped with orders for his precious ice, trying at the same time to build a lighthouse, he had no choice but to pull his men out of the search for the body of Martin Lang. And still he needed more help. Farmers, with nothing to do on their snow-locked farms, began to see in John Skandl their only salvation. They brought into town teams of horses — Percherons, Clydesdales, Suffolk Punches — to be fitted with the long, sharp ice caulks that crunched loud on the wide stretches of river ice. The endlessly moving teams filled the valley below Tiddy's house with the sounds of horses and men. The smell of horse shit and sweat filled the streets of the town, began to seep in through the closed windows of the newspaper office. Liebhaber struck back by printing in the *Big Indian Signal* a half-page account of the pro-phecy by Walking Eagle that the forthcoming winter would be the mildest since the disappearance of the buffalo.

Ice was the only thing in the world that Skandl really under-stood. Put the shit bags on the horses and plane down to black ice. Remove the chips with a team and scraper. Score the ice with a marker. Cut a gash with the ice plow, plow the field, cork. Skandl, on the river, and in his vision of himself too, shaping the perfect blocks, imagined himself a lover.

The open water steamed the air white. The horses, wearing their ice caulks, moved through the haze. And out of the crunched air, out of the pure white cloud, rose the tower.

It rose in the middle of the river, in the middle of the town. The stacked blocks of clear ice, each morning, shone with a new and abrupt glory. The ice of Skandl's erotic dream shimmered a translucent blue in the blank glare of what should have been a harvest sun. At a loss for words, he told a man to hold a watch to the rising wall; he walked around to the other side and read the time through a block of ice.

Liebhaber, in a fit of outrage at the endless bad weather, told a lie: he reported that a road north of town was alive, one afternoon, with garter snakes that had come out of hibernation. "Liebhaber is losing his grip," people said, over the tables in the beer parlor, over their bingo cards in the Elks' Community Hall.

The day after the snake story appeared in the newspaper, John Skandl was acclaimed reeve of the Municipality of Bigknife. At first he called no meetings of his councillors. In the fury of his passion for Tiddy he did nothing but elaborate his scheme: he spoke of nothing but wave-swept towers, scorning land structures of any sort. Some days he spoke of John Smeaton's tower at Eddystone, built entirely of granite, all the blocks dovetailed, each one weighing a ton. Some days he spoke of the Bishop Rock Lighthouse, occupying the most exposed situation in all the oceans of the world; he praised the Skerryvore Lighthouse, its profile a hyperbolic curve from the hard rock to the lantern base. He reminded his men of the hazards of building a lighthouse on the dangerous shores of Brittany, on the Fastnet Rock off the Irish coast. He told them of the Rothersand Lighthouse and the difficulties of its erection. He spoke confusedly of the lights of Ravenna and Messina, of the ancient tower that was the Pillar of Hercules. And all the while he ordered the blocks of ice hoisted higher, stacked, positioned. He had them sprayed with water that froze and welded them together. He surveyed his rising creation and ordered another round of blocks, another layer, another reaching at the rim.

There were those muttering few, wives and mothers, who saw the tower as a kind of tomb or monument. Skandl responded by calling a meeting, not of his councillors, but of everyone.

He had his granary pulled ashore to make room for the crowd. The voters of the Municipality of Bigknife, on a Saturday night in

December, converged on the lighthouse. Tiddy Lang and her mother drove into town with their horse and cutter. They stopped on the crest of the hill, where the road led down into the valley to the old railway bridge.

The tower, lit up from inside by Coleman lamps, glowed tall in the night, a golden column of ice. It was then that Tiddy's temptation not to love began to weaken. She stared at the glowing, tall tower, the vibrant tower, down in the valley. She had never seen anything so wondrous. "Isn't it beautiful?" she said to her mother.

"It's too sad," Old Lady Lang said. She shook her head, under her black shawl. She'd kept on her apron. She clutched, under her coat, in a pocket of her apron, her special ball of sorrow. "I don't want to think about it," she said.

9

"Every snowflake is a penny,"

Skandl commenced. There wasn't enough room inside the base of the tower for all the crowd. Whatever he said was whispered back through the arched doorway, to the people who pressed close outside.

"Every snowflake is money in everybody's pockets. The country is paved with money. The ice is thickening fast. We must work day and night. The orders are coming in fast..."

Twenty of Tiddy Lang's suitors were in the huge crowd. To a man, they joined in the applause. Only Liebhaber refused to clap; he tried to shout against the din of approval. Recklessly he shouted against the din: "I heard a flight of geese heading north."

Liebhaber's words, too, were repeated until they'd spread outside the tower. People began to laugh at the preposterous notion of geese heading north in December.

Skandl, tall, shaggy, huge as a horse on the small platform of ice, ignored Liebhaber.

"Secession," he shouted.

The crowd roared its enthusiasm, its growing sense of excitement.

"The time has come," Skandl said. "If the province of Saskatchewan won't give us support in the harvesting of this wealth, the province of Alberta will."

Liebhaber, alone, tried to shout against the confused roar of delight. He'd been trying for weeks, with no luck at all, to remember the future. He'd listened to weather reports on two radios at a time. He'd analyzed the color of the sky and studied, in sea shanties and navigational guides, the significance of sunsets and sunrises, an activity that led to his interest in the design and function of boats. Much to his own chagrin, he'd predicted the coldest night ever to occur in the Municipality of Bigknife in the month of November.

"Cowpie," Liebhaber shouted. "I found a soft cowpie. Somewhere, the grass is green."

"Horse shit," Skandl shouted back at him.

The laughter silenced Liebhaber. Skandl raged against the capitalists and the socialists alike, arguing persuasively for a change of the status quo. "The time has come," he repeated. He said again that ice would be the mainstay of the community. The crowd roared its agreement. Skandl called for a show of hands. The tower was full of shouting people, the women, especially, arguing against the ice; the men, most of them, rallying to Skandl's side, arguing that the lighthouse must be built taller, still taller.

In the babble and chaos of voices, Liebhaber, wildly, tried to undercut Skandl by arguing perversely in his favor. He pictured the tall lighthouse white against a black sky, its finger of light touching out, beckoning the very birds that no longer came to the municipality, bringing down from the high night the geese, the ducks, the robins, the crows, the meadowlarks, the orioles. Liebhaber, recklessly, in the endless winter, invented a spring.

While Skandl raved on about the catoptric versus the dioptric; yes, the time had come, he would construct the optical apparatus; he, the giver of light, mentioning in the same breath the Pharos of Alexandria, built in the reign of Ptolemy II, one of the wonders of the world; Skandl roaring, the other suitors roaring, the curlers waving their brooms, the mothers and wives in the crowd in despair now, silenced, hardly daring to listen...

Tiddy recognized that the men, in their desperate confusion, were trying to get to heaven. They must be stopped. She was trying to find words; Tiddy, who did not argue at all. She was trying to imagine words when she saw her second daughter pushing her way into the tower.

Rose Lang called in a loud whisper for her mother to come at once; a few people in the mob heard the single word, Vera. Tiddy, leading Old Lady Lang, began to push her way out of the chaos. She could hear Skandl, above the others, roaring and bellowing that the time had come. She heard the curlers insisting that Big Indian would shortly produce the greatest curling rinks in the history of the game. The fish peddler was pleading that more ice be cut, and faster; it must be cut and hauled from the surface of the lakes or the lakes would freeze to their bottoms; he'd found an eight-pound whitefish in a block of Skandl's perfect ice.

Tiddy wrapped her mother in robes and blankets in the cutter.

"It's too sad," Old Lady Lang said.

"Hurry," Rose said, finding room in the cutter beside her grandmother.

The lighthouse, behind the departing cutter, might have been on fire. People, years later, came to associate that strange beacon in the December weather, that fire made of ice, with the birth of Vera's boy.

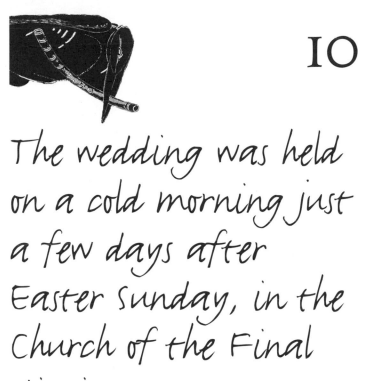

The wedding was held on a cold morning just a few days after Easter Sunday, in the Church of the Final Virgin. Why Tiddy Lang chose John Skandl out of all her twenty-four suitors was never explained to anyone's satisfaction. Father Basil, irked by Skandl's building a lighthouse that was now twice as tall as the church steeple, launched into a sermon that lasted one hour and ten minutes before he so much as mentioned either the bride or the bridegroom. He was stout and bushy-haired, the old priest, with eyebrows that curled down over his eyes. A myopic man who liked nothing better than a sip of homemade Hutterite wine, he was too vain to wear glasses; on one occasion he delivered a three-hour harangue to a deserted church, having confused Saturday and Sunday.

"Yesterday morning," he repeated for the third time, "I went out to start my car. I had to buy prizes for the bingo game." He paused. "Seasick," he said. "Bouncing. Seasick...Any fool could see that the car had..."

Puzzled, he turned to one of his altar boys.

"Square wheels," the altar boy whispered again.

"Square wheels," Father Basil reiterated, his breath freezing in front of his mouth as he spoke from the altar. The register over the furnace was in the aisle in the middle of the church. "The world," he announced, underlining his insight with the raised stillness of his cold-stiffened right hand, "lacks sufficient centrifugal force to maintain its roundness."

He raised his other hand out of the folds of his vestments. "Some of you good people bring in from your frozen fields reports of..."

He turned again to the two altar boys.

"Blue snow," they whispered together.

Father Basil cleared his throat of phlegm and swallowed. "Evidence. Blue snow is evidence. Direct evidence. The world is out of motion. We inhabit a strangled universe."

Liebhaber, seated in an upstairs pew where he might see through a window and watch the sky, was tempted to pray; he began to hope that Father Basil might go on through the morning, into the afternoon, talking on and on until the weather changed. He glanced over his shoulder, through the frosted window, at the sleighs in front of the church, at the cars, their hoods covered with horse blankets or old quilts. He faced again the altar where Father Basil spoke, where the bride and groom and the best man and the bridesmaid waited. He noticed Tiddy's hand, furtively touching Skandl's thick wrist; the couple, endlessly impatient before the altar. Liebhaber, even then, and almost not dreaming, in love.

Father Basil was connecting the presence of wolves in the district with the failure of the world to turn on its axis. "It's the lack of centrifugal force," he was explaining, "that enables the wolves to range this far south. Like the blue snow. Like my square wheels." And then, out of his own quiet, out of his hush, his motionless stance, he burst into motion, flailed his arms. "We've got to bust her *loose!*" He liked, on occasion, to use the language of his parishioners. "The sprocket wheel of being is jammed," he shouted. "The bull pinion of existence has jumped the heifer gear of eternity."

At that exact moment a great puff of black smoke gushed from the top of the lighthouse. Skandl had planned to have a light come on just as the wedding party arrived at Tiddy's farm; he'd designed a lantern that would give a light sufficient to show in the day. But something had misfired.

Tiddy saw, through a church window, the cloud of smoke like a huge, black bird bursting into flight. She started. She stepped back. In so doing she caught a spike heel of her white shoes in the hem of the long, loose dress she was wearing to disguise her pregnancy; she toppled down the single step.

Father Basil, seeing nothing, undisturbed by the confusion at the altar, went on raging against the weather.

Tiddy Lang, or Tiddy Skandl — and the controversy as to whether or not she was actually married was to rage for years — Tiddy made no sound. She collapsed into the folds of her dress. John Skandl picked her up in his arms and turned from the altar. He struck out, walking and running, toward the door of the church, toward his new Essex and a dash to the General Hospital.

.

II

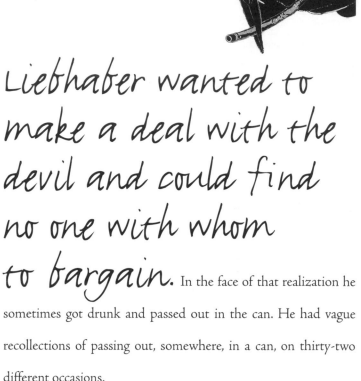

Liebhaber wanted to make a deal with the devil and could find no one with whom to bargain. In the face of that realization he sometimes got drunk and passed out in the can. He had vague recollections of passing out, somewhere, in a can, on thirty-two different occasions.

He spent the afternoon of Tiddy's wedding day in his flat above the newspaper office, studying his collection of wood type, puzzling with his ink-stained fingers the intricate knot of language that bound him to death. He hated most the large capital letters, cut from rock maple, mounted on blocks of wood for the convenience of some printer who had long ago himself been distributed back into the neat chaos. Liebhaber, simply in pain.

He liked to drink while he sat alone at his kitchen table and hated his collection of type. He tried, with the twist of a wrist, to turn an M into a W. Failing at that, he turned a T upside down; but he could read it as easily upside down as upright. He poured another shot of rye into a jar that still wore its bold label:

Robertson's Marmalade. He set the word OUT, building from the T he had tried to mock out of meaning. He left the T on the table. He placed the U on a windowsill. He carried the O into his living room. But he knew the word OUT was still OUT. It was the failure to reduce a mere three-letter word to nothing that made him attempt a sequence of illogical sentences; he printed across the linoleum of his living room floor: I'M NOT ALONE. REALLY. He ran out of punctuation. He found his apostrophes and periods, what few he had, in a shoebox under his bed. He concluded his trilogy of sentences with I'M NOT. Studying his accomplishment, he decided to make a new name out of his initials.

He decided to make the word GLOT and got up from the floor and went into the bathroom for a G and an L. He kept the Gs and the Ls in rows on top of the tank of his toilet, along with scissors for trimming his mustache and his nails. Accidentally, he sat down. He might have stayed there; he might have fallen safely and comfortably asleep, had he not smelled the smoke. He imagined the word WATER; then, in his mind, turned the W upside down. Liebhaber smelled the smoke, coming from the top of the lighthouse, out on the frozen river. He didn't stop to put on his camel-pile coat. Recklessly, he stumbled down the dark back stairs. He hurried, as best he could, through the snow-slick and deserted streets of Big Indian, down toward the river.

12

He was at the lighthouse when the hand touched the back of his neck, when the ghost touched him. He thought at first it must be Vera — Vera, disregarding her fine sense of decorum — come to reproach him. He was pissing on a hoof of the mare she had used to drive into town; she refused, ever, to ride with anyone. She rode only with her son, the baby wrapped in blankets under the robes, beside her on the cutter seat. Beside the baby she carried a rock, heated on the kitchen stove and wrapped in rags.

Liebhaber felt the hand at his neck. He heard the familiar voice that complained, "Freeze the nuts off an iron bridge."

Liebhaber recognize the voice, for all its new hollowness. But the night wasn't cold; he recognized that too. Wanting to die, he looked down to where the ghost's feet must be. The fingers that touched him were colder than the night. He could see nothing. He looked. He could see nothing.

"I saved you," Liebhaber whispered. He knew he was lying. But he was pleading too, asking for simple mercy. The grip of the invisible hand tightened. But even in that gesture it was gentle, not threatening, and Liebhaber hated its hesitation. He fumbled to button his fly. "I did my best," he insisted. He leaned against the quiet horse. It was the same black mare they had ridden together, the two men, out of this same town. "I tried," Liebhaber said.

And then he heard the ice. It cracked clean and hard, like a snapped bone. Distantly at first. Then the cannon thud of the heaved ice boomed through his legs. Liebhaber turned from the stirring horse. He dared to turn.

Martin Lang looked lonesome. That was all. He stared for a while, into Liebhaber's face, with eyes that were full of loneliness. He was about to speak again. His right hand was raised toward Liebhaber. He dropped his hand and turned and limped toward the lighthouse.

The wind was blowing hard. Martin Lang was having difficulty, walking in the wind. It was blowing hard and warm and dry, a chinook, come suddenly from the southwest. The snow was melting. The river was rising.

Liebhaber shouted after Martin Lang, "Hey! Wait a minute!" The black mare, tied to a post that was frozen into the shifting ice, jerked at her halter rope. Liebhaber followed Lang around the tower, toward the arched doorway.

Someone had built a campfire in the base of the lighthouse. Two dozen men, more, were sitting around the fire on blocks of ice. The mounties were likely to show up for a wedding dance in the Big Indian Elks' Community Hall; the dancers had concealed their bottles of rye and their cases of beer in crevices in the walls of ice.

Vera Lang was talking softly, her small son asleep in her arms. She was asking the idle men to do something about the smoke that poured down from the top of the lighthouse.

Somewhere in the night, alone at the farm, Vera had realized the weather was breaking. The smoke that blanketed the town, that spread out over the river flats, was certain to harm any bees that had survived through the winter; we must tell the bees, when they come out, she was explaining. We must tell the bees what happened. She gestured out at the night. She spoke softly, then, of a queenless hive, of mating, and the men didn't understand. She was so arrogantly beautiful, Vera, that the men wouldn't argue. But they did not understand either. They watched the light on her polished face. "And the drones," Vera went on. "The males. After the nuptials." She rocked her child, gently, in her arms. "The males are useless…"

"Is Martin Lang here?" Liebhaber asked.

The men in the tower burst out laughing. Liebhaber had saved them from the seduction of Vera's cold, fatal beauty, and from the pain of her words too. They were only men. They laughed in pleasure at their own laughing. They could talk now, stand up, stretch, cough, spit, fart, laugh, holler. Someone gave a holler, out at the night.

Leo Weller, reaching behind a block of ice, produced a bottle. The imprint of a horse shoe, stamped on his forehead, shone in the light from the campfire. He rubbed the palm of his right hand across the top of the bottle of rye and offered Liebhaber a drink:

"It's a new record, Leeb, for the General Hospital. Born twenty-four minutes after she left the church."

"If you can't be good, Leeb, be careful."

The men were teasing him now. They ignored Vera. "Tiddy always wanted a son," someone said. "If you can't be careful," someone said, "name it after me."

A block of ice plummeted down from the dark tunnels over their heads. The smashed ice exploded over the small fire. The loafing men bounded into their own sudden fear: the thunder of cracking ice rolled up, slammed into, the hollow tower. A strip of black water opened at the tower door.

The rear runners of a sleigh fell into the open water. Two men struggled briefly to unhook the panicking horses; one horse slipped threshing through the ice, pulled the other along; the team plunged trumpeting into the icy water. But no one stayed to help. Drivers spun their cars across the ice, into the cover of smoke. Other teams, in terror, lost in the darkness, smashed sleighs and cars together.

The ice around the opening water was soot blackened, as black as the water. The wall of the high tower cracked, began to crumble, as Liebhaber, leading Vera and her child, found the cutter. Choking in the smoke, his hands and face smeared black with soot, he reached for the mare's head; he unsnapped the halter rope from the halter. Vera was in the cutter, holding the reins, pulling back on the reins.

Liebhaber leapt to a runner, hung on for dear life to the back of the cutter. He was trying to talk to Vera, trying to tell her where to go, when the runner hit a rock or a log. Liebhaber, there beside Skandl's old granary, was flung into a bank of wet snow.

Vera Lang drove alone with her son through the confusion of cars and sleighs and people on Main Street, in front of the Elks' Community Hall. The orchestra went on playing; the wild notes of a trumpet tore at the night. A pall of black smoke hung in the street. She slapped the reins against the mare's flanks. She drove toward the bridge that would take her safely across the river, up out of the valley.

It was then, hardly beyond the bridge, driving through the stand of poplars and spruce where the road began the ascent up the side of a coulee, that she saw the first wolf.

The pack was following Vera Lang. The timber wolves were closing in. Already, the thaw was making the road sticky, with bare spots showing through the slush. The old mare had difficulty, trying to run uphill in the slush, over the bared clay ridges on the rutted road.

Years later, the people of Big Indian would agree that Vera Lang did the right thing. She was left with no choice. The wolves, working methodically around her, closing in on the spent horse, on the lone woman, the small child, were winning; they would, in a matter of minutes, in another two hundred yards, have their victims.

Somewhere above the town, on the edge of the clay-shouldered trench that was the valley of the Bigknife River — and by then she was dazed out of all the surmise, out of all sense of direction — somewhere, almost reaching the snow-blank plain, Vera of necessity threw her son from the cutter. He fell into the darkness behind her like one last snowflake, in the March night. If he cried at all, Vera's boy, not one person heard.

13

John Skandl, on the night of the chinook,

sitting slumped and disheveled in his new blue suit and shirt and tie on the edge of Tiddy's bed in the Big Indian General Hospital, began to explain why he must immediately leave town: it was his duty to his constituents. He made no mention at all of his lighthouse, or of its vanishing. He must leave, he explained, because culverts would wash out. Grades would wash out. Bridges would be weakened. A program of road building and flood control was essential. He resolved to anchor himself to the earth. It was important, vital, that the provincial government construct a main highway into the heart of the municipality so that, in the future, when calamity struck, assistance might easily reach his beleaguered people. He left the hospital and went directly to his icehouse; he boarded a freight train that was hauling a shipment of blocks of ice into the city.

Tiddy, one week after the night of the chinook, took her son home from the hospital. JG, as John Gustav soon came to be called, was the most beautiful baby ever born in the Big Indian General Hospital. He was too handsome to look like anyone. Perhaps he bore a slight resemblance to Tiddy. But there was one complication nevertheless: when he cried he made no sound, a condition of silence he was to maintain throughout his life.

Fortunately, the chinook that ushered in the spring signaled also the return of the birds to the municipality, among them, the black crow.

It was simply there one morning, perched on the foot of the baby buggy. Tiddy had placed a dishtowel over the buggy to shade the baby's eyes; a gust of wind had lifted it away. Liebhaber — it was mid-morning; he'd fallen asleep in the old easy chair on Tiddy's porch — Liebhaber awakened and saw the crow perched on the buggy, its head cocked, staring at the baby, the baby, his eyes open, staring at the crow.

That same crow and Liebhaber, the two of them together, soon came to be regarded as the laziest pair of creatures in the district. There were not enough people in the whole community to attend to all the fence fixing and calving and repairing. Seeding followed hard on the tilling and harrowing; there would soon be summer-fallow to look after, haying to be done. Since Liebhaber did much of his typesetting at night, he was seen every day loafing his way toward the farm.

The only thing he could do well around Tiddy's house was sit with JG. Tiddy's younger daughters quickly became bored with looking after the child, for he didn't make a sound; he never offered in return for attention paid the pleasure of a single gurgle or cry, a possible word. Instead, the beautiful face looked around forever innocent; only the black crow fascinated the boy.

The crow perched on the back of a chair for hours. Sometimes it sat on a gatepost, by the untrimmed caragana hedge, and cocked its head at the condescending remarks of visitors. Occasionally it hopped on the ground, to peck up a bug or a seed, but mostly it preferred to be fed from its special dish on the porch. Liebhaber soon came to address his remarks directly to the crow, rather than to the inattentive baby, complaining bitterly that Tiddy was whimsical, persnickety, high-hatted, stuck-up and a blue-eyed terror. Sometimes he raised his voice, hoping to be heard inside the house as well. But Tiddy ignored his every insult and entreaty, his every cry of pain.

She was a married woman again, and as such she was suddenly the most proper creature in the municipality. Skandl wrote her a letter six weeks after his departure. His duties in the capital were proving to be more demanding, more arduous, than he'd anticipated. He explained at considerable length that while he realized it had been, traditionally, the obligation of the municipality to build roads, he was attempting to make it a provincial responsibility. He proposed a great network of roads for the Municipal District of Bigknife. The prairie trails would lead into graded roads. The graded gumbo roads would join gravel roads. Those gravel roads would lead to paved highways of the kind he'd heard were being built in other countries, on other continents. He, personally, would be responsible for all contracts. He would, if the government didn't accede to his wishes, go through with his secession plans.

Meanwhile, one old farmer with a four-horse team and a grader was attempting to maintain the ruts and washouts. Vera Lang, especially, complained; she had to travel, all spring, over those same roads with her horse and buggy, setting up and attending to her apiaries. She found out where the first buds appeared, sticky, in a poplar bluff. She came to know where caraganas first scented the air, where crocuses bloomed on a bare hillside. Then, her apiaries established, she was equally busy, adding supers to the hives, watching that the bees didn't swarm, warding off ants and mice, checking, always checking, for disease and ruin.

Liebhaber couldn't decide whether to love or to hate Vera. One afternoon she drove into the yard while he was tending JG, talking to the crow. She was wearing a bee veil on the brim of her straw hat, a pair of beekeeper's gloves, a new pair of white overalls that concealed in layers and folds of cloth her entire body. Liebhaber became infuriated.

She was pretending not to possess the beautiful but mortal body that had once been naked to the bees. Liebhaber wanted to explain that to the crow. He enjoyed explaining things to the silent, attentive bird; he had a few statements he wanted to make about vanity and desire.

"The whole country is bitched," Liebhaber began.

Vera went to the rear of the buggy and lifted her hive tool and her smoker out of the way. She found in the box at the rear of the buggy an empty gunny sack.

The gophers were so thin, after the endless winter, that Vera had taken to feeding them when she went on her rounds; she stopped to feed the gophers that darted out, gaunt, almost starved to death, tattered and scruffy, onto the rutted roads.

"Our friend Vera…" Liebhaber resumed, rather pompously.

And that was the first time the crow spoke. People, years later, insisted that it learned to talk from listening to Liebhaber piss and moan about the world. He was always pissing and moaning, people said. Whether or not the crow was speaking what was on the silent child's mind, that was never clearly determined. But there were those who insisted that the black crow sometimes spoke on behalf of JG.

"Liebhaber," the crow said. It had never spoken before that moment, had hardly bothered to say caw. "Liebhaber, you don't know your ass from your elbow. You are a *Dumbkopf* beyond my worst expectations. Don't you *see* what our friend is doing?" The talking crow was always, thereafter, to be a champion of gophers; there was always something of a bond between gophers and crows. "Why," the crow went on, almost sarcastic in its hoarse way, "don't you go out to one of Vera's bee yards, take off your right boot, hook your dirty big toe onto the trigger of a borrowed shotgun, and hope for the best?"

After that there was no keeping it quiet.

14

As the summer wore on, as Vera became preoccupied with the harvesting of honey, Tiddy found herself totally strapped for help. Liebhaber decided she must somehow afford a hired man and by advertising he managed to locate an unemployed veteran who'd lost his right leg and his private parts in what he referred to as an English war. His name was Mick O'Holleran, and while his disability limited his usefulness on the farm, Liebhaber felt it was more than compensated for by the security he provided in a household made up of a grass widow and six unmarried young women.

When the second daughter, Rose, announced one evening at the kitchen table that she was pregnant, Liebhaber demanded that they hold a family council at once. He'd arrived, as was his wont, a few minutes after supper was put on the table. The council was held over raspberry pie topped with whipped cream, and lasted for a total of three minutes. The canning season was in full swing, the kitchen cabinet was heaped with cobs of corn and cucumbers, the boiler on the stove was full of quart sealers. The women were in a hurry. O'Holleran, without the slightest argument, admitted that at times he not only felt the presence of his missing leg and private parts, but could actually use them.

Rose Lang blushed. She was as homely as Vera Lang was beautiful. It was a graceful kind of homeliness. People who couldn't remember the names of the Lang sisters referred to Rose as the homely one and were never misunderstood.

Rose Lang had a passion for burying dead birds and making novenas for their souls. During the year of the endless winter that at first gave her many birds to bury and then, later, almost none, she'd begun to bury broken cups and saucers in the snow, and with the return of summer she had not reverted to her earlier custom. Dead birds were scarce — a baby robin fallen from too high a nest, a pigeon or sparrow caught by a cat and not devoured before the cat was in turn caught by Rose, a partridge that had smacked into a telephone line. Broken dishes were plentiful in the Lang house. Rose began to include soup bowls and dinner plates in her cemeteries, setting little crosses in the earth beside the graves.

She and O'Holleran wanted to get married. The younger girls in the household forgot all about making bread-and-butter pickles and corn relish; they began to wonder who would be bridesmaids, who would give the shower, who would play for the wedding dance. Liebhaber felt such embarrassment at his failure in judgment and leadership that he went back into Big Indian and swore he'd never again set foot outside the town. He stopped playing pocket pool for a total of thirteen days, and during that time he hit on the notion that he might evade death by telling the truth.

Sitting alone in the composing room at night, surrounded by shadows and softly outlined machines, the smell of ink and kerosene strong in the air, his small light closing him in its own glove, he began to compose absolutely true accounts of events; he would print only one copy before distributing the eight-point type back to its comforting chaos. His quick hands working, he could in a single night record an event, run off a single copy on the Miehle press, then break the type back into the Hamilton drawers again. By the dawn of each day, when he prepared to go to bed, he was himself hardly more than a mere tray of alphabet, awaiting the insistence of an ordering hand.

Bent over his drawers of type in the long night, Liebhaber tried to remember the future. But he remembered nothing. He knew it was Gutenberg who'd made all memory of the past irrelevant. He heard, instead, from the basement below him, the squeaking of Zike's bed: Zike, downstairs in his basement room, fucking his head off. That was Zike's way of putting it: "Fucked my head off last night," he would say to Liebhaber, while the flatbed printing press made such a racket that Liebhaber, unthinking, would ask him to repeat what he'd said. "FUCKED MY HEAD OFF LAST NIGHT," Zike would shout in his ear, with no further comment by way of boast or apology. Sometimes, Liebhaber, in the long night, setting type, would hear a muffled squeal of surprise, a giggle. And then, the giggles forgotten, he'd hear the taking of pleasure, the rhythmic moans of pleasure, the cries of love. He couldn't endure it.

Tiddy — only Liebhaber thought of her as Mrs. Skandl; everyone else in Big Indian went on calling her Tiddy Lang — stayed on the farm as resolutely as Liebhaber stayed in town. Sometimes the cows mooed. Sometimes they didn't. Sometimes the chickens laid. Sometimes they needed oyster shells. Sometimes the thistles or the pigweeds grew faster than the wheat. Sometimes hail fell instead of rain. Sometimes the dust blew through closed windows. Tiddy, with her hardheaded radiance, held together the past and the future. Her daughters went on maturing. Her mother grew older, more wrinkled, forever clutching her ball of sorrow in a pocket of her apron. JG was more work than all the others, all the other conundrums of the world, put together. He grew larger. He said nothing. Tiddy accepted his existence as she accepted the stinkweeds, the grasshoppers, the green grass in spring, the sun. She learned to talk to JG's pet crow, learned to give answers and take them too. Perhaps Liebhaber missed the farm.

One morning he left the composing room and went as usual up the back stairs to his flat. He stopped in the doorway amazed: his rooms had been cleaned. A pot of coffee was ready on his old cook-stove. His bed was made. All the capital letters in his collection of wood type were set in neat rows, arranged alphabetically. He couldn't bear that either. In terror at the domestication of those free, beautiful letters — no, it was the absurdity of their recited order that afflicted him: ABCDEFGHIJKLMNOPQRSTU VWXYZ — he opened a twenty-six of rye and, with immense effort, tried to disentangle himself from the tyranny of rote. The U, he argued aloud to himself, in the Middle Ages, was the final letter, held by the wisest of men to be only a rounded version of V. He tried to resay the alphabet and failed. I and J, he remembered, were once deemed the same: he tried to disregard one in his recitation and lost both. He tried again, the simplest changing of the alphabet — and heard himself making sounds for which he had no signs all.

At ten-thirty that morning, Liebhaber passed out in the can. He was convinced that Tiddy, in her merciless search for husbands, had persuaded the alphabet itself to become as inflexible as her original wish and command: Someone must take a wife. That evening, just in time for lemon meringue pie and coffee, he showed up at the Lang farm.

He'd figured out a way to make Tiddy rich and independent by developing a new breed of cattle. He'd set stories about the need for a dairy cow suited to the rigors of the northern climate; Tiddy was persuaded by his arguments and statistics to name the new breed in his honor, Liebhaber. That was all he expected in return.

Now the pages of the *Big Indian Signal* were full of reports on Polled Durhams and Herefords, on Guernseys and Jerseys and Holstein-Friesians. Liebhaber, ahead of his time, wanted to bring in the Charolais and the Limousin breeds from France, the Simmenthal from Switzerland. He talked of nothing but milk production versus meat production, of grasslands and feed lots, of diets and cream prices and the future of cheese and the color of milk. Tiddy put a lot of money into purchasing breeding stock and remodeled her barn. Liebhaber began to conduct experiments in artificial insemination in order to speed up the genetic process. He invented gadgets for the collection and dissemination of the semen of widely scattered bulls. He argued with Father Basil about the souls of cows. He bought bib overalls to wear over his ink-marked clothing; he bought rubber boots and began to smell of cow manure.

The long-range effect was simple: years later a government inspector informed Liebhaber that he'd perfected the three-titted cow. The immediate effect, however, was more disastrous: a young man from a neighboring farm, Nick Droniuk, was hired to help out with the herd while Liebhaber was absent. One day, watching a teaser cow excite a bull, he become so excited that he accidentally inserted himself in the semen-collecting device. Anna Marie, Tiddy's third daughter, was assigned to mix the semen with egg yolk, than to measure it off into quantified units for insertion, with a pipette, into various breeds of cow. AI-ing, this was called, to Liebhaber's immense satisfaction. Hardly two months after Nick's initial experiment, Anna Marie made her announcement. They were sitting around the kitchen table, the women. Rose was grating potatoes, preparing to make potato pancakes. Vera was reading a new book about bees. Tiddy and Old Lady Lang were shelling peas, both of them sitting with their legs slightly spread, the unshelled peas cradled in their laps on their aprons. Rose's baby girl was all wrapped up and asleep on the lid of the woodbox. Anna Marie, by the sink, was combing her hair. "It's snowing," she said, smiling slyly.

Anna Marie was a tall, gangling girl with thick, wavy black hair that she combed for hours on end. She had long irked her sisters with the elaborateness of her hope chest. In addition to the usual towels and sheets and embroidered pillow cases, she had accumulated a variety of charms and aphrodisiacs. Her hope chest was stuffed full with dried flowers and mushrooms, birds' feathers and the wing of a magpie, a variety of small stones, a dried pigtail, a leather pouch full of horse hair, six gopher tails, a dozen crows' eggs that she'd blown out and packed in an empty cigar box.

She and Nick Droniuk were married on the day that Rose and Mick O'Holleran baptized their second baby girl. It was a joyous occasion on the farm: neighbors came from many miles away. A number of farmers from north of town, all of them Nick's relatives, stayed at the farm for three days, drinking moonshine and eating and dancing. Anna Marie and Nick, unable to escape the festivities, had their honeymoon in the loft of the big red barn.

Liebhaber, during the celebration, came to understand that to withdraw from society was folly. He could delight in the arguments, if need be, along with the songs and laughter. The moonshine was tolerable. It was an autumn wedding, and the gardens yielded up no end of fresh peas and new potatoes and corn on the cob and tomatoes so huge they were bursting out of their own skins. He resolved to embrace mankind.

That winter, Liebhaber agreed to be a referee for the local hockey league. Tiddy warned him: she said he didn't have the legs for the job. That made him all the more determined.

Tiddy's farm, at the time, was thriving. Her granaries were bursting with wheat and oats and barley. Her new dairy cows, while they produced little milk, had given birth to excellent veal calves. Tiddy sold a dozen calves to a cattle buyer who flirted with her outrageously for four days.

It was to be the first night game in Big Indian: they'd just installed enough lights to make a night game possible. The play was rough. Liebhaber, as referee, removed yet always there, watched the disputes, the hard checking, the high sticking, the errors, the affections and disaffections of the swarming, eager players. The rougher the game became, the clearer his vision. He was some kind of arbitrator, the civilizing man. He liked that. The civilizing man: at the center, and yet uninvolved. The dispassionate man at the passionate core, witnessing both jealousy and desire, separate from either.

The Big Indian Braves were playing a team from south of town, as typical a collection of thugs and ruffians as might be found anywhere on a skating rink. How the fight got started was uncertain: within thirty seconds there were twenty-four players on the ice, gloves off, smashing at each other's faces and heads. Liebhaber took out a pad of paper and began to write down names: Weller, Krystofiak, Evans, Morgan, Messner, McGill, Campbell, Wolbeck, Martz, Congdon, Badry, Kroetsch, O'Connor,

Strauss, Kramer, Van Slyke, Kuntz, Zimmer, Fankhanel, Ross, Tomchuk, Thibeau, Biganek, Lassu. But it was Gladys Lang, jumping onto the ice, who confused the list: he accidentally wrote down Martin Lang.

Gladys loved to throw a ball against the wall and catch it when it bounced back. She was like that in adolescence, and had been from early childhood. Some days the endless thumping of a ball against Tiddy's bedroom wall, against the barn door, against a granary or the car shed, nearly drove the others insane. When Gladys was upset, or happy, or depressed, or merely bored, or something else, or nothing, she took her ball and went outside and began to throw it and catch it. When she saw the puck lying unguarded on the ice she wanted to pick it up and throw it against the boards and see if it would bounce for her, see if she could catch it.

Thirty or forty spectators, men and women alike, tired of heaving chunks of snow and ice from the heaped snow around the outside of the rink, jumped over the boards and joined the fighting. Much of the population of Big Indian was on the ice, kicking, flailing, bashing, screaming, crying, jerking, beating.

Liebhaber was the hero. He walked over to a box on a post by the skating rink shack and turned out the lights. He was able, that night, single-handedly, to assert order. After he turned on the lights he gave eighteen penalties and called the remaining six players to a face-off at center ice. Only three people had to go to the hospital. The game was finished without further incident, the Braves winning by a score of three to two.

For the next few weeks, Liebhaber settled all differences, on the ice or in the skating shack; he dealt out justice; he won outstanding praise for his objectivity and fairness — he, that same Liebhaber who only recently had been alone. He was quite simply the patriarch: a man who deserved to have a large family, friends, visitors, admirers. He began to feel a condescending pity for poor Gutenberg, crazy as a bat in a curious way, obsessed to the point of self-destruction; old Gutenberg, dying childless, penniless, friendless, anonymous, almost not invented into his own story. The cattle-buyer had vanished, like a character gently removed from the vast novel that all the printers in the world were gallantly writing for Gutenberg's ghost. Late one night, sitting at the Linotype machine that Mr. Wills had acquired second-hand from a newspaper in the city, Liebhaber hit on the notion that he might avoid Gutenberg's fate by making a few autobiographical notes. *I am become my own legend*, he typed on the big machine; he was secure, there in the night, the matrices falling into place at his command. *I perish. But only in a dream...*

A knock at the door surprised him. Reluctantly, he stood up from his low chair. He was still new to the machine that had replaced his composing stick; but he found the heat of the melting lead a consolation. He stepped from his small ring of light.

Outside, the wind was blowing; for a moment he closed the door again, against the driven flakes of snow.

"Gus?"

The voice called through the closed door.

"Gus? Is that you in there?"

Liebhaber, in love. Stricken again, by the darkness itself. He hated to be interrupted in his work. He was chewing a corner of his mustache; he felt for his mustache, there in the dark. But he heard the voice, and knew it.

"It's about Gladys."

"Is that you?" he said.

She was out there in the wind, in the snow: Tiddy Lang. Tiddy Skandl.

He thought of the letter O, from his collection of wood type. He tried to let it become a mere circle. A cat's eye. The perfect circle of a soap bubble. He would free the O from the O, let back into the world the zero of ought. A spinning coin. The inside of a robin's nest. The white and lifted host in the priest's right hand. The absolute of Tiddy's breasts.

"It's about Gladys."

"What about Gladys?"

"The night of the big fight," Tiddy said. "At the skating rink."

Liebhaber was angry. He was outraged. Liebhaber, the man who had given them justice, truth: goddamn goddamn. "Fuck!" he shouted. Not a violent command; an outcry, rather, at the deceit of the world. The world's deceit of her wistful fools. "It's impossible!" he shouted.

"Yes," Tiddy answered. "It's true."

Liebhaber, groaning aloud, hammering his raised fists against the closed door, shouting: "Who's the father?"

Tiddy opened the door. Liebhaber, swinging his pain-torn body against the place where the door should have been, fell out of the newspaper office, onto the sidewalk, into the snow.

"Everybody," Tiddy said.

15

That was the cause of the schmier game — the inadequacy of truth. Liebhaber showed up at the farm, on the following Sunday morning, an hour earlier than usual; he begged Droniuk and O'Holleran to play a couple of hands of schmier before dinner. Tiddy had already told Anna Marie to stop combing her hair and to set the dining room table.

"One game," Liebhaber argued. "I'll do the dishes after we eat."

"One game," Tiddy said. "At the kitchen table. We're to eat in forty minutes."

She wouldn't have made that mistake had she not seen the neighbor, Isador Heck, walking down the road behind a team of horses. She moved the two flapper pies and a loaf of fresh bread off the table, onto the kitchen cabinet. She sent Cathy down into the cellar for some jars of corn relish and dill pickles and a quart sealer of sausage.

Isador Heck was the most eligible bachelor in the district. Unfortunately, he was laughed at by many people for his skepticism: he claimed to believe in nothing. When he broke a big toe by dropping a post maul on it, he healed himself by disallowing the theory of gravity. He refused to go to Mass because of an argument he'd had seventeen years earlier with Father Basil over the nature of light. Father Basil argued that light was the white corpuscles of the universe. Heck argued that light was the absence of dark. He lived in a homestead shack in the middle of a section of hay sloughs and windblown wheatland and had never swept his floor, speculating that if anything did in fact exist, there was no reason to believe it was visible.

When Isador came into the yard, intending simply to borrow a hayrake because his had broken down, Tiddy asked him to stay for Sunday dinner. Isador at first disputed the assumption that the day was Sunday, or indeed that any day was anything but a day, assuming it was that; then he saw the three men playing schmier and having a bottle of pilsener at 11:30 in the morning. In spite of his principles, he took off his greasy tweed cap with a greasy hand. "Deal me in," he said, ignoring Tiddy.

Liebhaber was shuffling the cards. It was that precious Sunday time, after church and before dinner; he was hurrying, but luxuri- ating too, free of his anxieties as Tiddy's daughters flourished all about him, mashing the potatoes, finding clean linen napkins, looking for the gravy boat, serving up pickles and whipping fresh cream. "Ten cents a game," he said, "and a nickel a hickey."

"Bid out or sneak out?" Isador hung up his cap on top of Tiddy's best coat, pulled a chair back from the table

"No sneaking out." Liebhaber dealt each man three cards at a throw, then another three.

"Move your feet," Vera said. She was trying to sweep under the table. Vera, polished as bright as stone, was furious at her mother for allowing the game to begin, furious that Isador Heck had been invited to stay for dinner.

Droniuk looked at his cards, peeked at them one by one, then looked over his shoulder at his wife, then closed the six cards together and cupped them in one large hand. He'd wet his hair, to try and make it lie flat, and it stood straight up. He had a deuce for low but only queen for high. "Two," he said.

O'Holleran looked at his cards. "Beats me." He rapped his artificial leg with his knuckles, indicating that he would pass.

Heck seemed to bid without picking up his last three cards from the table. He nodded to himself. "I'll risk it for three." He looked to Liebhaber.

"A good setting hand." Liebhaber rapped the table. "Shoot."

Half an hour later Tiddy asked the four men to come into the dining room to eat, the food was hot. But they wanted to finish the game. Liebhaber had three hickeys. Heck had four. O'Holleran had sixteen points on the back of a leaf from a calendar where Liebhaber was keeping score, five more than he needed to win. But he couldn't get the bid.

The four men were playing racehorse schmier, playing only the suit that was bid, in order to speed up the game. They were trying to hurry. O'Holleran shuffled and let Heck cut; he dealt quickly; the men looked at their cards and bid quickly. The black crow was perched on the back of an empty chair, setting its head this way and that, watching the game.

Heck held back his jack of spades when he should have schmiered against the bidder; Droniuk caught it with the queen on the next play.

"Dummy," the black crow said. It had been perfectly quiet up until then. "Dummy," it said to Isador Heck.

Isador Heck had spent many days of his life trying to kill the crows that hung around his farm. One time he fell out of a tree while trying to rob a crow's nest and was left hanging for two hours before the branch finally broke. He fell and was knocked out for another two hours and for weeks he refused to believe that the afternoon wasn't the morning. Another time he tried to shoot a crow that was eating with his chickens and accidentally he shot his only rooster. He didn't believe in crows.

"Jack and game," the black crow said. "Jack and game."

Heck, flustered, picked up the cards and began to shuffle before Liebhaber had recorded the points. He set the deck in front of the crow as if to let the crow make the cut. "Asshole," he shouted at the crow.

By three o'clock the four players were so hungry they asked for a cold sandwich or something, whatever they could eat while they played. Tiddy was losing patience. She agreed to give them a bite if they'd move out of the kitchen, into the dining room, so the girls could clean up the dinner dishes before it was time for supper.

JG, in the parlor next to the dining room, was able to watch the game leaning over the bottom half of a Dutch door. JG sometimes filled his pants: it was almost the only way in which he could express himself. In the excitement of watching the game, at having so many men present in the room next to his, he jumped up and down and waved his arms. The smell of his shit began to permeate the dining room. The game might have ended then, when Tiddy served the cold beef sandwiches and the pickles and more beer, had not Ken Cruickshank arrived. He drove into the yard as Liebhaber bid four on ace and deuce, hoping to catch the jack and keep game when he led with the ace.

"Asshole," the black crow said.

Cruickshank, the barber and pool hall operator, was a widower. Tiddy met him at the door.

"The men are playing schmier," she said. "Why don't you sit down and have a glass of my chokecherry wine. They'll be finished in a minute."

Cruickshank was seated at the kitchen table, sipping a glass of chokecherry wine, when he heard Liebhaber begin to swear at the cards and at the black crow. Cruickshank kept as many as a dozen punchboards in his barbershop. Liebhaber had made two points on his four bid; he was, in this game, twenty-seven points in the hole for a total of nine hickeys.

"Asshole," the black crow said.

Cruickshank put down his half-empty glass. "Excuse me," he said to the women. He took off his hat and hung it on the back of the kitchen door, next to Heck's greasy cap, and went into the dining room.

Mick O'Holleran, when it came time to do chores, for the first time in his life refused to go out and feed the pigs. He was the most reliable man in the district. He said he'd milk the cows just as soon as he got his three dollars and ten cents back: his initial good fortune had taken a turn for the worse.

Isador Heck was arranging coins and bills in neat stacks between the elbows of his greasy denim jacket. He'd been raking hay when his rake broke and had tried to fix it out in the field. His hands dirtied the cards, the coins, the table.

"Move your feet," Vera said. She was trying to sweep up in the dining room.

Vera Lang hated Isador Heck for his slovenly dress and his unbearable ignorance. Sometimes, when he'd had a few beers, he argued against the existence of a world beyond the municipality. Why pay taxes to build roads, he argued, when there's nowhere to go? Vera hated the dirt that was caked in his ears. She hated the sweat stains in the armpits of his dirty workshirts. She hated the smell of manure on his boots. The trouble was, he sometimes grew huge fields of clover. Vera's bees loved clover.

Rose O'Holleran, at seven that evening, slipped on her husband's rubber boots and picked up the two slop pails. Later she was to see that as her first error. She should have spent the evening burying the serving plate that Rita accidentally broke while trying to write a letter on the kitchen table.

Rose asked Anna Marie to stop combing her hair and to lend a hand with the chores. The house was in shambles; it was almost a pleasure to go outside and feed pigs, to walk through the chicken coop and find a few warm eggs under the hens, to sit milking a cow, listening to the warm milk zing into the pail. But Rose managed to stayed just a little bit angry, putting the cows in the pasture, lifting the heavy pole gate, while her husband played schmier. Sometimes Rose's anger made her beautiful. Anger did that to Rose, and she had come to realize it; she wanted to get to bed early.

Sometimes when there were chores to do, Gladys went out and bounced her ball. She was throwing the red rubber ball against the cellar door, trying to make a double hit, off the slanting wooden door and the wall too, before making a spectacular catch. The men, trying to concentrate on their cards, listened for the inevitable bouncing of the ball. "Why don't you find her a husband?" Liebhaber called to Tiddy. He had never spoken to her that way before.

"Why don't you lay an egg?" Tiddy called back to him.

But then the chores were done; the women of the house sat at the kitchen table and talked for a while. Vera nibbled daintily, delicately, at the small bones in a chicken neck. Rose's older daughter, Theresa, delayed in every way her having to go upstairs to bed. Old Lady Lang watched over the two sleeping babies, Rose's and Anna Marie's; she poured a drop of whiskey into her coffee. It was a pleasant hour, the men in the dining room, out of the way, playing cards, opening another case of beer. The gray covers from the tall brown bottles became gauntlets for JG: Cruickshank slipped them onto the boy's wrists. JG sulked when he was told he must go to bed; the black crow assured him there'd be a morning. "Tomorrow will be just as miserable as today," the black crow said. Sometimes there were weeks when it said almost nothing.

After a while only Old Lady Lang and Tiddy were left at the kitchen table. They talked of gardens and babies and sewing. Sometimes they said nothing at all. Old Lady Lang was slightly irked at the men for using her deck of cards. Once or twice she reached into the pocket of her apron, fondled her ball of sorrow. But only briefly. It was haying time, and the days seemed so long, so endless, there could be no urgency in the world. Even at ten o'clock, the northern sun glowed faintly in a blue rim of sky. Night sounds, when the men were stilled into concentration, came gently from the slough beyond the barn; a slough pumper, a fussing of mallards.

Cathy Lang was the only one absent. By the time she arrived home, at three in the morning, the game had been in progress for twenty hours. Shoes in hand, she was tiptoeing across the kitchen floor, waiting for her mother's inevitable call from the dark bedroom, "Is that you, Cathy?" But she heard, instead, the men playing cards. It was their very obliviousness to her presence that made her speak.

Cathy, the youngest of the six sisters, was the normal one. All her life she'd heard it: after the wild glory of her older sisters, she heard, always and again, "You're the normal one, Cathy. Thank heavens." They said it with such enthusiasm, her relatives, her friends, her mother, her sisters themselves. But no one ever explained.

Cathy put her head in at the dining room door.

"I'm in love," she whispered.

She wanted to tell someone. She had expected to be caught only by her mother, and now she had an audience of five stern men.

"Hey!" she whispered. "I'm in love."

O'Holleran, out of politeness, not looking up from his cards: "Who with this time, Cathy?"

"Joe Lightning."

The five men at the table might have been frozen stiff, they were suddenly so without motion.

"Not the *Cree* Joe Lightning?" Liebhaber said.

"Of course," she said. "There's only one Joe Lightning."

Not one of the men spoke.

Joe Lightning was the champion shuffleboard player of the entire district. He was a small, young, ferociously handsome Cree from the reserve to the north of Big Indian. He would gamble on anything. All day he played shuffleboard in the Big Indian Hotel; at night he lived in a car body behind Gordie Somer's garage.

"There's no such thing as love," Heck said. He started playing again.

"I'm in love," Cathy said. She wanted the men to see that her hair was a mess. She'd been necking. "I'm scared shitless," she added.

They wouldn't look up. The five men wouldn't look up from their cards, they peeked each at six cards, meditated, weighed the possibilities. Cruickshank glanced at the piece of cardboard, ripped from the top of a cereal box, that Liebhaber was using now to keep score.

"Two." Droniuk brushed at his stiff hair. He had the deuce for low, but only queen for high.

O'Holleran knocked the table with his knuckles; Cruickshank shook his head and swore.

Heck scratched the smudge of wagon grease on his forehead. "Goddamn," he said. "Pass," he said. "Good setting hand."

"Three." Liebhaber led the king of diamonds.

"Asshole," the black crow said.

16

By nine o'clock the next morning word of the game had spread to neighboring farms.

Leo Weller, a pig farmer, and Eddie Brausen, a young fellow who was himself in love with his cousin Cathy, almost drove into each other, turning their cars in at the Langs' lane. The men at the dining room table made room by carrying in the bench from the kitchen. At this point Liebhaber had thirty-one hickeys in a game that had commenced at six AM. By eleven that morning the seven players realized they were becoming unnaturally thirsty. They broke straws from Vera's broom and drew to see who would go into town and pick up a keg of beer. Liebhaber lost: he was back by noon with a keg of cold beer in the back of Art Van Slyke's car. Van Slyke, a grain buyer who ran the Pool elevator, had nothing much to do that day; he thought he'd sit in for a few hands of schmier.

Tiddy didn't mind too much. She felt it was a time of year when farmers should take a few hours off. Granted, there was summerfallow to be worked, hay to be mowed and stacked; but mostly they were waiting for the wheat to begin to head out and fill and ripen. It was a pleasant time of year. She sent her daughters out to pick beans, to shell peas, to thin the carrots and the beets, to dig under the potato stalks with their bare hands in the cool earth, for small new potatoes to be washed and then fried whole in butter. She creamed the peas and carrots; she went down into her cellar to the sauerkraut crock and then made up a kettle of sauerkraut and backbone; she pulled enough rhubarb to make three pies.

It was either late Monday night or early Tuesday morning when Bill Morgan and Alphonse Martz arrived together; they were no longer working for John Skandl. They had gone back to farming. They came almost furtively, remembering the trip they'd made by sleigh to retrieve Martin Lang's frozen corpse from the night and the snow. Morgan, his empty eye socket slightly moist, was careful not to look out of any window that would give him a view of the clothesline. Martz's slight deafness caused the other men to raise their voices. "Deef," Martz would say. "Speak up," he would say when he didn't understand something. "I'm deef in one ear, and I can't hear out the other."

Tiddy, for all the inconvenience, for all the strain she was putting on her pantry, expected to find at least one husband. Even on the third day it was not she who complained, but the black crow. It was becoming indignant, jealous. Tiddy realized that the women were running the world better than had the men; she was content to let them go on with their game of schmier. It was the black crow who began to sense the desperate nature of the playing. Some awful pressure that the men themselves did not understand was holding them in thrall. The black crow took to flying over the table, flapping up awkwardly into the air, then landing on a player's shoulder, then kibbitzing, mocking: "Scared? Scared shitless?"

"Why don't you learn to caw?" Leo Weller demanded of the crow. He was a tall, lean man with the outline of a horseshoe printed on his forehead, where a horse had kicked him when he was a boy. The scar made a shiny reddish U on his forehead, the color of mahogany. He was an uncle, by marriage, to the Lang sisters; he loved the six sisters as much as he hated the crow. "Just learn to caw."

"Scared?" the black crow said. "Scared, Uncle Leo? Scared shitless?"

"*Caw caw,*" Eddie Brausen said. He was showing off for Cathy's sake; he raised his head, chin out. He'd lost the middle finger of his left hand while clearing a chip from the blade, while sawing wood, and he cupped his right hand over the fingers that held his five cards. "*Caw caw.*"

Ten of the men played at a time, each player receiving five cards. They'd put the two jokers into the deck. There were four cards sleeping in any hand played; the bidding was vicious.

"Bid," Liebhaber said.

"Three."

Leo Weller passed. "Bid 'em high and sleep in the streets."

The black crow hopped away from the back of Eddie Brausen's chair, onto Bill Morgan's shoulder. Morgan was pouring beer from the pitcher into his glass; he tried to shake the crow away. He'd lost his left eye in an accident in a grain elevator. The crow tried to peck at the empty socket. "Bugger off," Morgan said. "*Caw.*"

"Bugger off," the black crow said. "Bugger off."

The cawing attracted JG to the doorway of the parlor. The small wooden gate wouldn't have stopped him for a moment, had he tried to break it down; but he never tried. He stood at the gate, his handsome face as youthful as ever, his face that showed not a sign of aging. JG was eternally young. His cheeks were pink, under the slightest down. His eyes were blue. He was the handsomest young man in the district, by far.

Rita Lang heard her brother stirring and came into the dining room from the kitchen. She was carrying her writing tablet and a pen. She didn't want anyone to see the letter she was writing. "JG," she said. "Be quiet. Go play with your puzzles." Rita turned from JG to the crow. "Tell them to bugger off," she said.

"Rita," Tiddy called from the kitchen. "Watch your language."

"*Caw caw*," Eddie Brausen said. He was in love with his cousin Cathy and hated Rita. Cathy didn't like Rita either, and was always finding excuses to leave the house. Eddie Brausen had round shoulders and he was somewhat defiant of the crow.

"Bugger off," the black crow said.

"*Caw caw caw*," Leo Weller said. When he became excited the U on his forehead seemed brighter than ever. "If somebody doesn't strangle that fucking crow, I'll do it myself."

"Just as soon as I win," Liebhaber said, "I'll help."

"Win," the crow said. "Win." But its hoarse voice changed as it repeated the word. "Win?" the crow seemed to be saying. It cocked its head, looked brightly at Liebhaber. "Win? Win? Somebody's going to win?"

Even O'Holleran, for all his common sense, was tempted to argue with the crow. He was embarrassed at not having shaved in days. He looked around to make sure Rose wasn't within hearing distance. "*Caw*," he said.

Isador Heck shook his head, wiped a greasy hand across his grease-marked forehead. "This isn't happening," he said.

Droniuk stretched his neck of a sudden, tilted his eyes up at the ceiling. "*Caw caw caw caw caw caw*."

JG's face broke out laughing; he made not the slightest sound, but his handsome face was laughing: all the men at once turned to the crow, to the laughing boy: "*Caw*," they were shouting. "*Caw caw caw caw caw caw caw caw caw caw caw caw caw caw caw caw*."

Rita Lang, at that moment, swung all her allegiance to the side of the crow, against the players. She hated them. Each evening, she was in the habit of sitting at the dining room table and writing letters. When she read in the *Big Indian Signal*, in the farm weeklies, of a man being sent to prison, for any crime whatsoever, she sent him a letter. She wrote erotic letters to those imprisoned men, spoke of her longing, of her dream of their thin, suffering bodies, of their pale hands. She caressed their thighs with words, she kissed the hairs of their bellies. She had no other admirers, no lovers, only those men whose names she found in the newspapers. And she never opened the letters she received. If there was a name and address on an envelope, she sat down at the dining room table and sent a reply without reading the letter. She added the unread message to her hoard, slipped it into one of the shoe boxes she kept numbered and ordered under her bed.

Liebhaber hated her for those unread letters, those secret, unopened letters. They tempted him to imagine what desperate pleadings they might contain, what longing, what despair. Liebhaber too, with the other players, was lifting up his head, making himself hoarse with the single cry, "*Caw caw caw.*"

"A bunch of raving idiots," the black crow said. It flapped away in disgust, into the darkened parlor, to sit with JG.

Rita bent down behind Alphonse Martz's chair. He'd fallen into a well when he was a boy. When the searchers finally found him and got him out he was perfectly fine, except that his hearing was impaired. He had, in a single night of darkness, up to his neck in water, down in the well, learned silence. A doctor told him he had willed his not hearing and therefore couldn't be helped by medicine. Father Basil prayed for him and that hadn't helped either.

Rita, pen and tablet in hand, stooped behind Alphonse's chair, behind his head. She'd approached him unheard. She touched her fingernails to his neck, like the claws of the black crow; Alphonse Martz started wildly in his fright and flung his cards over the table.

17

Almost four weeks to the hour after the game started, Tiddy finally lost her temper.

All the women of the house went to Mass that morning. All the men refused to go. While the women were out of the house, Isador Heck got the black crow drunk. He gave it beer to drink, in a dirty ashtray, and when Tiddy walked unexpected into the dining room, the black crow fell off the back of a chair and sprained a leg.

Tiddy was furious. "It's time the whole lazy pack of you went to work. Skidaddle. Scat. Bugger off."

"Conniption fit," Liebhaber said. He had a good setting hand and didn't want to be interrupted. "Don't throw a conniption fit over a few hands of schmier."

For four weeks they'd been playing on her dining room table. Day and night they played, ignoring the weather, ignoring time, family, duty, season; ignoring everything but their one passion. Sometimes a man slept for a part of a day or night, went away for an hour or two: but there was always an extra player, waiting to sit into the ten-man game. The cases of empty bottles and the beer kegs so cluttered the entry that the Lang girls could hardly get in with pails of milk. The children, in the evening, had no place to play with their coloring books and their cut-outs, no place to do their homework.

By two o'clock that Sunday afternoon, the black crow had a raging hangover. It was dying of thirst.

"This is an outrage," Tiddy said. "I'm going to go hire the Hutterites."

Yet, even then, she was not so much angry at the men as at her two youngest daughters, Rita and Cathy. She'd hoped they might show some interest in the younger players. Instead, Rita mooned around all day, sullen and angry because she couldn't use the dining room to write her letters. The pure sensuality of desire aroused and denied had become her greatest pleasure; now she herself was its victim. She thought of her prisoners, everywhere, forgetting her, learning to dream of other women. Cathy mooned around all evening, dreaming of Joe Lightning; he would play shuffleboard until ten o'clock; then, after the beer parlor closed, he'd show up on his horse, in the garden. Tiddy had smelled the horse smell on Cathy, and knew it was serious love. But, hearing a horse neigh, going to her bedroom window, she would see only her husband, on his plow, plowing the snow.

The schmier players were beginning to look seedy, smell seedy. JG was becoming unmanageable, the black crow was impossibly insolent. She was making a drop of broth for the hungover crow when it shat in the middle of her kitchen table.

"Shame on you," Tiddy almost shouted at the crow.

"Shame on you," the black crow said.

At that moment Tiddy turned to where Vera was polishing her face in front of the mirror over the sink and asked for a ride to the Hutterite colony, at the southern end of the municipality. No one gave a thought to Vera Lang those days. "Let's go," Tiddy said.

Monday morning at eight o'clock, with the dew off the wheat, the Hutterite men came onto the farm with their binders and their four-horse teams; they were short, bearded men in black hats and black clothing. They spoke softy to each other in a German that was their own secret language; sometimes they spoke secretly with Old Lady Lang. She remembered a few words like *Scheisskopf*, *Schweinhund*, and when she used them the Hutterite men looked toward the house and laughed. They worked hard from dawn to dusk, cutting the wheat and oats, then stooking. Sometimes, in late afternoon, two or three of the older men found an excuse to head into town, to the almost deserted beer parlor. But at suppertime they put their horses into Tiddy's barn, piled into the back of an old truck and drove home to eat and sleep.

One of the young men, beardless, one evening came by the house to ask which field they were to cut next. Gladys was throwing her ball against the wall of the house, outside the dining room. Gladys had reddish hair like her mother and delicate breasts with nipples that were almost the color of gold; anyone could tell that, watching her throw the ball. Tiddy was in town, buying groceries so she could feed her gang of card players. The young man went into the dining room to wait.

That's how it happened that Eli Wurtz was in the game the night Old Lady Lang read fortunes. He'd been playing for a week, resisting every order from the Hutterite wheat boss that he return to stooking. No one could understand why he stayed in the game, because in a whole week he hadn't won a single hand. He'd look at his cards; "*Du* son of a gun," he'd say. He was clean shaven. He took pride in his black trousers and jacket and his bright green shirt. His black cowboy boots were always shined. He never took off his straw hat.

Liebhaber, by this time, had dropped out of the game seventeen times, gone back to work for as long as two hours, and returned seventeen times. Isador Heck lost his entire hay crop without ever cutting it. Leo Weller, short of money one day, had bet and lost all the posts in a mile of barbed wire fence. Another man had bet the roof of his house while on a little losing streak.

It was on the night that Cruickshank won Heck's team of horses that Old Lady Lang started reading fortunes. The horses were still in Tiddy's barn, from the Sunday of his arrival to borrow a hayrake; Tiddy's daughters watered and fed them twice a day. Old Lady Lang sometimes sat in for a hand, to spell off a player who had to run to the barn to relieve himself. She was playing for Liebhaber when she turned up his five cards and gasped.

It was a little before midnight. Liebhaber had actually gone not to the barn but to the car shed. Tiddy was trying to end the game by refusing to allow any beer in the house. The players slipped out one or two at a time to the car shed, took a quick pee in the dry weeds behind the building or in the sawdust behind the woodpile, then ducked through the car shed door to find a bottle of beer cached in the old washing machine, in a rubber boot, in a discarded tire, in the trunk removed from the rear of the old Essex that had once been Skandl's.

Liebhaber returned to the game in time for Old Lady Lang to show him his hand: four queens and a joker. It was a useless hand as far as schmier went. "So what?" Liebhaber said.

Old Lady Lang shook her head. "*Ach*," she said. "It's too sad. I don't want to think about it."

Liebhaber wasn't satisfied with that answer.

"You're going to die of love," she said.

"Bullshit I'm going to die."

"You're going to die in this house," she said.

The other players laughed. "We're not going to stay that long," Eddie Brausen said. He concealed his missing finger.

Liebhaber took the cards from Old Lady Lang's hand, asked her to move, and sat down. But he couldn't bring himself to bid. That was the first time, really, that he recognized the seriousness of their game. He tried to explain to others. "This is a serious business," he said. When they laughed again, he asked Old Lady Lang to look at their cards.

One man was holding a pair of jacks and three threes. Another held five hearts, from the ace to the five spot. Another held three one-eyed face cards. Old Lady Lang looked and shook her head, "*Ach, ja*." The men, moving the coal oil lamps so they might see better, looked anew at the worn cards, at the worn numbers, the worn pictures. They had never seen their cards in quite that way before. Old Lady Lang, looking at one man's handful of spades, refused to comment. They could hear, from the parlor, a sound of regular breathing. Sometimes JG fell asleep on the chesterfield. The crow, in the dark room, muttered something to itself. The house creaked.

They knew, those men, studying their cards in the presence of Old Lady Lang, they knew there was no meaning anywhere in the world.

"My husband," Old Lady Lang said, "was a fiend for a deck of cards."

"Yes," Leo Weller said. "I remember."

The other men in the room fell quiet.

"He was playing once," Old Lady Lang said. "Here. At this table. With Leo's father. With Eddie's grandfather. Some others too…Homesteaders, all of them."

She gestured toward the windows. They looked, the listening men; they saw only the darkness, beyond the reflection of themselves in the bright glass.

"He went outside to go to the outhouse. It was dark already." Old Lady Lang broke the deck into two halves and riffled the cards. "He was walking…There was still a poplar bluff where the car shed is now…Where you keep your beer.

"He heard some men coming down the path…The path to the outhouse…He stepped, into the poplars."

She was talking so much she made a mistake. She was dealing herself into the game, leaving one man out. The waiting men glanced at the awkwardly distributed cards, each man trying to decide which might be his.

"He looked in once. They were carrying a coffin. He looked into the coffin."

She had finished dealing. The coal oil lamp gave off an inadequate light. She had in her hand the four cards of the missy, the buried cards. She put them face down on the table, beside the next dealer.

"He came running back into the house…He had no breath. He could hardly tell us…

"It was himself he saw in that coffin." She was arranging the cards in her left hand, studying the cards. As dealer, she would get the last bid; she was ready to wait. "In the bed beside me. In that bed where you were, Gus…Next morning." She glanced impatiently about, waiting for the men to pick up their cards, to bid. "When I touched him. Even before I touched him. I could tell. I could tell by the weight of him, there in the bed."

18

That same night the schmier players moved their game to Isador Heck's tarpaper shack.

Heck left the dining room while Old Lady Lang was in the parlor, shushing the black crow. He harnessed his horses in the dark and led them out of the barn; he hitched onto a doubletree and carried the doubletree, behind the team, to the pole of Martin Lang's big wagon that had the green tank box on it, for hauling grain. Leo Weller was the next man out of the house. He found a lantern in the barn, cleaned the globe with a page from the *Big Indian Signal*, and struck a match.

It was Leo Weller who hit on the idea that they might continue the game while driving. Two of the men spread a binder canvas on the floor of the wagon box — the Hutterite men had finished cutting and were about to start threshing — and Leo Weller put down the lantern in the middle of the canvas. They started out through the dark night, the players, over the rutted road.

Halfway to Heck's place, Alphonse Martz said, "Eli, it's your deal."

They looked around, groped beyond the lantern's circle of light.

Eli Wurtz was not there.

The players had their first real disagreement. Some of them wanted to turn back; they missed Tiddy and her concern. The others remembered Old Lady Lang's dark eyes, peering into the blank depths of a deck of cards. They asked what she had said, to silence the black crow.

"*Schwarzkopf*," Art Van Slyke said. "All she said to the crow was *Schwarzkopf*."

"She's no fool," Liebhaber said. He was surprised to hear himself defending the black crow. But he couldn't stop himself: "She told me…"

"*She?*" Andy Wolbeck interrupted. "What the hell do you mean, *she*? What is this *she* stuff?"

Then the men were arguing again; their voices, in the dark, floated up disembodied from the moving wagon. They couldn't agree on the sex of the crow; Eddie Brausen said it had a filthy, wicked tongue for a woman.

"All she said was," Art Van Slyke shouted, trying to shuffle the cards, "was *Schwarzkopf*."

Isador Heck's tarpaper shack was worse than a pigpen. It was almost daybreak by the time he'd unhooked the horses and fed them; he said he'd make a batch of pancakes. He stood at a shelf by the dirty kitchen stove, mixing batter while the other men got the card game going. The heat from the stove warmed the flies alive. Heck scooped them out of the batter almost as fast as they fell in; he flicked flies and bits of batter against the greasy wall with a dirty finger.

"Raisin pancakes," Eddie Brausen said, when Heck put the first pancakes and the Rogers' syrup can on the table.

The houseflies, all day, were so thick that sometimes the players had trouble seeing their cards. Night was little better: at night the millers and moths swarmed into the two-room shack as if to put out the men's eyes. The whole place had a sour smell. By dawn of the second day, most of the men had diarrhea from the bad water and the sandwiches made of greenish bologna.

Going outside was almost worse than staying in the shack. Heck had nailed rotting coyote hides and dead hawks to the walls. Gophers and snakes abounded, right up to the doorstep. The barn hadn't been cleaned in months and the manure was so deep that no one could enter there to relieve himself. Outside the barn, the carcass of a dead horse stank to high heaven. Sometimes, when the wind blew from the wrong direction, the stench of death spread through the shack itself; the men were barely able to continue the game, some days, some nights, against the impediments. They were losing weight because Heck insisted on doing all the cooking, his pots and pans and plates as dirty as his hands. They could barely bring themselves to eat, the players. And yet they knew they must not only go on playing; they must win. Old Lady Lang had seen that about them. The black crow had seen it; the consequences of not winning were too terrible to contemplate. Andy Wolbeck reassured the others by remembering out loud the disappearance of Eli Wurtz. He tapped his toes.

The only clean objects in the place were the toes of Andy Wolbeck's right foot. He was the station agent in Big Indian, though his wife and children did all the work. One time when he was drinking, on a bet he let a train run over the tip of his right shoe. He now wore artificial toes, perfect toes, carved from old billiard balls. He took off his right shoe while playing cards; the tap of his toes on the floor, like a claw, sometimes irritated the other men. But the toes were perfectly clean.

They played right through threshing time. On a quiet evening they could hear, in the far distance, the hum of a tractor. The fine chaff drifted across the flat, sunburned fields; it drifted into the clumped poplars. It drifted into the rings of willow that marked the sloughs where ducks fattened, preparing to head south. It drifted into farmhouses, where busy women cooked for the threshing crews. It drifted into the small towns, where wagons and trucks, loaded with wheat, lined up at the grain elevators. At sunset the western sky was red, the sun itself muffled by the drift of chaff in the motionless air, by the far hum of machines.

The filth in Heck's shack was offensive to Liebhaber. The blankets and bedsheets on the cot were so dirty, so gray and black, that most of the men went out, when they had to sleep for a few hours, and climbed up into the hayloft. The trouble was that pigeons, in the cupola, or perched on the sling rope that looped through the center of the loft, for hoisting hay into the barn, tended to shit on the sleepers. Liebhaber quit the game six more times.

Sometimes Liebhaber sneaked back to visit Tiddy, instead of returning to work; but now he was himself so dirty, so exhausted, so totally unattractive, that Tiddy wouldn't even offer him a cup of coffee. She stood behind the hooked screen door and continued to be polite. Except that on one occasion when he surprised her with a visit, she inconsiderately placed her left hand over her nose. Her blue eyes watered.

Zike kept the newspaper going. He was a twicer, able to work at both case and press, and Liebhaber hated him for it. Zike worked day and night, hardly finding time to go down to his basement bed where women came secretly in the night, because Zike was an albino and with Zike it didn't count. Which sweethearts and wives of the schmier players found their way down his barely lit steps, no one ever knew.

It was Liebhaber, returning to Heck's tarpaper shack for the sixth time, bringing fresh bologna and a few loaves of bread, who brought word of the wedding.

Joe Lightning and Cathy Lang were to be married the next morning. Cathy had fixed up the car body so they might both live in it behind Gordie Somer's Garage. Joe was winning regularly in various shuffleboard competitions across the prairie provinces and down into Montana and North Dakota. They were marrying for love.

Eddie Brausen was so badly hurt by the news that he put down his cards on the table. He refused to play when it came his turn. The other men began to argue violently against his silence;

no person in the municipality, ever, they explained, had married for love; Liebhaber must, again, be mistaken. Eddie shook his head. Andy Wolbeck and Leo Weller at once began to cite instances of neighbors who took wives to avoid cooking or to grow their own help or to get another quarter-section of land. Eddie only shook his head. Bill Morgan and Alphonse Martz and Ken Cruickshank together named thirteen girls who got married because of the back seats of cars, one who wanted an indoor toilet, three who hated having to do the milking. Liebhaber himself couldn't resist arguing, even if it meant disputing his own assertion. The game was at a standstill. He argued vehemently that lust and sloth alone were the reasons for matrimony; he defied any man in the room to name a single person, in the whole history of the Municipal District of Bigknife, who married, who would marry for anything but lust or sloth.

"Cathy and Joe," Eddie said.

The men didn't believe it. They had to go see for themselves. They went outside, all the players together; to their surprise, the ground was white. Snow had fallen, during the night; a bitter wind was blowing from the north.

Heck went to the barn and brought out his team. The card-players climbed into the wagon box, then decided to move the big green box onto the sleigh bolster. They had no warm clothing. They huddled together, their fingers so cold they couldn't play while they traveled.

They looked like a pack of scarecrows. Almost all of them were coughing. One or two at a time, they leaned over the side of the sleigh box, spat into the snow. They farted, and their farts almost warmed them. Their assholes were raw and bleeding from the combination of diarrhea and prairie hay that was full of thistle and buckbrush. They tried once or twice to sing, but then Alphonse Martz cursed instead, pointing to a magpie that hopped off the road, away from a dead rabbit. The magpie began to follow the sleigh; it was joined by another magpie, then another.

"We're surrendering, aren't we?" Eddie Brausen said. He was in pain at the thought of Cathy's wedding. He was too young to know when to lie.

"Surrender?" Liebhaber said. "To what?"

"To the women."

"Never."

"The women will be there, won't they? At the church."

"*Caw*," Liebhaber said. He tried to frighten the magpies away by shouting. "*Caw*."

"*Caw caw*," O'Holleran added. He had a bad cold and was so watery-eyed he could hardly see the windmilling magpies; he could hardly recognize their careful patience as they bounced down onto the road in front of the gaunt team, the load of scarecrow men. O'Holleran felt guilty.

"*Caw caw caw*," Droniuk shouted, hoarsely. He tried to smooth down his hair; he brushed at his unshaven face. "*Caw caw caw caw caw*," he shouted. He felt guilty.

"*Caw caw caw caw caw caw caw caw*," the men said now, not so much to the waiting magpies, as to each other. They huddled together, the sleigh moving slowly through the frozen morning.

19

How they happened to deal the first hand, there in

the basement of the Church of the Final Virgin, was simple enough; Eli Wurtz was the cause. "*Du* son of a gun," he said when he saw Liebhaber looking more scarecrow than man.

Eli was standing on the church steps, out of the wind, with Gladys Lang on his arm. He was dressed entirely in black, from his black hat to his cowboy boots, except for a bright green shirt. She was dressed as a Hutterite wife, her red hair, in its coif, concealed under a flowered scarf. Her long-sleeved blouse of flowered navy blue cotton almost matched her flowered green apron. Her shoes, under the hem of her long black skirt, were simple and sturdy and black. She was smiling, radiant with joy.

Eli, the men in the sleigh realized, had not been playing schmier to win. Eli, obviously, had believed for so long in the communal good, he was almost useless in a card game. He'd been in the game, day after day, night after night, in Tiddy's dining room, because of Gladys. She'd been pregnant then. Now she seemed within hours of giving birth.

The players, rebuffed by Eli's merciless smile, went down into the basement of the church to get warm by the furnace. The basement had never been finished; the homesteaders who built the wooden church had simply dug a hole in the bald prairie that was big enough to contain a furnace, a coal bin, a stack of firewood. Someone has stored the church picnic tables and benches in the space between the furnace and the coal bin. Leo Weller set one of the tables upright and made a careless attempt at wiping the surface. Isador Heck was dealing before the others had found blocks of wood large enough to serve as chairs at the ends of the table, where the benches didn't reach.

The women were upstairs in the church, gathered around the register in the center of the aisle, above the furnace. They let the hot air warm their legs while they chatted about the weather and asked after each other's health. They spoke of the early snow and hoped it wouldn't stay. Some of the farmers west of town hadn't finished threshing: the schmier game had delayed everything. One woman wanted to say a rosary, after the wedding, for the souls of the players.

Newcomers, stamping on the floor to knock the fresh snow off their boots as they entered the church, shook ashes from the spiderwebs in the basement down onto the players. A fine grit of ash fell over each player as the church filled: a handful of Indians, solemn and quiet, filed into the church and sat together in two back pews.

Tiddy Lang arrived. She became the center of the group standing on and around the register. The heat scorched the legs of those directly over the furnace and they moved away, the church beginning to smell of hot rubber, and traded places with those who were shivering. Vera Lang was there: cold-eyed, imperious, she came in after her mother: when the others spoke of marriage, she spoke of her crop of honey. The bees had been busier than ever before. They'd filled one super in a single day. Now and then they glanced, all the women at once, toward the door: they awaited the arrival of the bride and groom.

The church bell rang. The impatient women, after a moment of hesitation, began to scatter away from the register, towards their family pews.

The men at the picnic table, in the basement, were on the verge of relenting. They might actually have gone upstairs, under cover of the ritual and the tolling bell, had not the basement door just then opened. It was hard to see, against the sudden light. The stranger closed the door, seemed not to have entered, then came down the darkened stairwell.

The stranger opened his black overcoat. He was wearing a dark, pin-striped suit, a white shirt and a red tie. He blinked, then saw the men gathered around the picnic table, the motley crowd of men, bewhiskered, dirty, shabby, haggard from lack of sleep, sick. He stepped to the furnace door, pulled off his black leather gloves, held his pale hands to the heat.

"Gentlemen, let me introduce myself," he began. "I'm Marvin Straw. Official hangman for your government."

The players hardly looked up from their cards.

"I came here to attend Rita Lang's wedding."

Liebhaber was writing the score on a shingle. "O'Holleran. Three in the hole. Martz. Low. Van Slyke. High and game. Cruickshank. Did you save the jack?" He glanced up at Marvin Straw. "It's not Rita Lang's wedding."

"It's Cathy's wedding," Eddie Brausen said.

"Damn." Marvin Straw banged a closed fist into the palm of his left hand. "Damn," he said. "Damn. Damn. Damn. Damn. Damn."

He'd come all the way from Prince Albert, from the federal penitentiary, he explained, just so he could go back and swear to Jerry Lapanne that Rita was married off and forever out of the picture. She'd mentioned a marriage, vaguely, in her last letter.

"It's Cathy's wedding," Eddie Brausen said. He looked at his cards. "She's marrying Joe Lightning."

Again, Marvin Straw went on with his explanation, compelled to speak to the indifferent listeners: a woman named Rita Lang kept writing letters to Jerry Lapanne, about to be hanged for murder. He'd escaped from maximum security four times. And each of those four times he'd made a beeline for Big Indian and the Lang farm. Each of those times the RCMP had been waiting at the Big Indian bridge, had captured their man and returned him to maximum security before he got so much as a glimpse of the woman he loved.

"Sit down," Leo Weller said. He brushed the ashes from the shape of a horseshoe stamped on his forehead. "You might as well play a hand of schmier before you head back. I got to go wring out my sock."

"Can't stay," Straw said. "Can't stay." Then he sat down.

Only after the third hand did Liebhaber begin to realize how desperate the situation really was. Marvin Straw went on talking while he tried to play the game. He played the wrong card, the wrong suit. Jerry Lapanne was to be hanged in three days. At dawn, three days hence. Straw, out of the goodness of his heart, wanted the man to die, if not happy, at least relieved of his passion.

Straw hated to lose. When he paid out thirty-five cents, he stood up to leave. He was buttoning his overcoat when, upstairs in the church, Father Basil began his sermon. Liebhaber signaled Straw to sit down and play another game; they must be quiet.

"God is our jailer," Father Basil, upstairs, his voice almost breaking with the cold, was intoning to his hushed congregation. "In the name of the Father, and of the Son, and of the Holy Ghost."

The effect in the basement was uncanny. Liebhaber, at that instant, for the first time in his life, cheated at cards. He withheld an ace and Marvin Straw, finally, counted two points.

Father Basil launched into his newest theological argument: after forty years of thought he'd decided there was a God, that God had created the world. Working a six-day week instead of the five-and-a-half schedule that was common in Big Indian, because of the Wednesday half holiday, He'd managed to create the entire universe, with the possible exception of comets.

A couple of the men at the table had noticed Liebhaber's gesture: and they too began to understand. A man's life was at stake. Liebhaber could hardly go on playing; he could think only of the morning three days hence when a man named Jerry Lapanne would hang by the neck until dead. Unless the hangman himself failed to keep the appointment.

20

Cathy Lang and Joe Lightning were happily become man and wife.

The fortunate couple were first out of the church, followed by the bridesmaid and best man, followed by the relatives, followed by the congregation. It was never determined why Father Basil left the wedding party and went to stick his head in at the door of the basement. Perhaps he was simply cold and wanted to get warm; the heat from the register, somehow, never got to the altar of the church.

Why he went down the steps into the dimly lit basement, that too remained, years later, a matter for speculation. One theory had it that, out of a Christian impulse, looking down on the bewildered, sick, desperate men gathered together around the dusty picnic table — out of nothing less than the goodness of his heart — he sent two altar boys to bring food and drink from the Elks' Hall, where the Royal Purple ladies were serving dinner. Another had it that he saw all the money on the table and assumed he might, by sitting in on the game, pay off the church debt, a debt which had been growing for fifteen years, largely because of the speculative nature of his sermons. A third had it that he was simply shocked at seeing some Protestants in the basement of the Church of the Final Virgin.

Father Basil sat down on a block of wood at one end of the picnic table. Marvin Straw was at the other. The eleven additional men were scattered wherever they might find room either to play or to watch. All tried to stay within reach of the jug of Jordan's Challenge at Father Basil's elbow.

They all understood now — all except Father Basil — that they must keep Marvin Straw interested in the game until three mornings had gone by.

By the first dawn there was no humor left in the players. They were playing to win, and to win they had to lose. Marvin Straw could hardly tell a heart from a diamond. But any time he hadn't won a game in a couple of hours, he was ready to jump into his car and drive back to Prince Albert and to his duties as hangman.

"Try one more hand," Liebhaber insisted.

"Can't stay," Straw said. "Can't stay." He picked up his five cards, got the bid. He led with the jack.

The men around one side of the table, each in turn, pretended they had nothing higher and folded shut their held cards.

Old Father Basil thumped down his queen on the jack, gave a hoot of satisfaction.

"Four escapes," Leo Weller marveled for the fifth time. "You were saying he climbed into a coffin?"

And Marvin, once more, was distracted from the old priest's winning. He began to tell again how Jerry Lapanne took the place of a corpse in order to escape the penitentiary and was almost buried alive. Or how, another time, he worked for two years, ate 420 pounds of brick and stone in order to conceal the evidence of his contrived escape, and then had himself captured within three hours because he made his usual beeline for Big Indian and the mysterious letter writer, Rita Lang.

It was Rita Lang who inspired his exploits. A single letter from her was enough to make him leap a twelve-foot wall, cut his way through barbed wire, dig a tunnel. Those same letters, now, in their distant way, had set a tableful of men to cheating desperately at cards.

By the second dawn they were hungry and thirsty. The food and wine from the wedding table had run out. No one dared leave long enough to go for supplies. They were running low on fuel. Even the spiders that had come down from the rafters were fewer, as the players began to be careful with wood and coal. The mice that had squeaked were silent, except when they rustled a scrap of paper or some shavings; their protecting woodpile grew smaller by the hour. Bill Morgan and Alphonse Martz broke up an old pew and a stack of folding chairs into firewood.

Now Marvin Straw was winning. He had on the table in front of him more money than all the other players put together. They had to win from him, sometimes, to recover money, in order to go on losing. Straw had taken off his tie; his suitcoat was smudged with ashes. The weight of time was enormous on everyone's shoulders. The light of day seemed fixed below the horizon; it would never peek in at the small, dirty windows, set into the foundation that rested on bald prairie.

They had not slept for three days and nights, the assembled players. It was almost dark in the basement, even during the afternoon; at night the holy candles, brought down from upstairs, hardly lit the cards. The figures playing the game were lost, each of them, in shadows beyond the edges of the picnic table. Father Basil, having run short of ready cash, charged ten cents each for the squat candles in their colored glass containers. Dawn threatened, and the players were reluctant to part with more dimes for more light.

The players had surrendered their identities to the need to keep Marvin Straw playing. Only one man was different: one player, over and over, beginning to win now, in spite of everything, would mutter to the others, "If the dog hadn't stopped to shit…" And then he'd slam down a winning card.

They had two hours to last, the players, to make Marvin Straw late for his hanging. He was becoming more restless by the minute. He'd have to drive like a madman, he complained, to get back to the Prince Albert Penitentiary in time. The exhausted men shook their heads in feigned sympathy.

In fact, a few were ready to let Jerry Lapanne hang. Straw was gaining ground against their resolve. Perhaps Lapanne is guilty, they whispered among themselves, when Straw stepped into a corner of the basement to relieve himself. But remember Rita Lang, others whispered in reply; we owe it to Rita, to her mother.

And that made Liebhaber think of Tiddy again. He was trying both to forget her and not to let the memory slip from his mind as he shuffled the worn cards. He dealt around the table. He ran out of cards before each player held five.

"Check your hands," he said. "These damned cards are getting stickier by the minute."

"Deal again," Art Van Slyke said. He was trying to be conscientious. "Nobody can count tonight."

Liebhaber gathered the worn cards together and shuffled again and asked Eddie Brausen for a whorehouse cut. It was nearly six in the morning: the hour of the scheduled hanging would soon be safely past. Liebhaber was beginning to fear that the sun would never come up, the night might be endless. He picked up the cut deck off the table, dealt.

Again he was short one card. He was certain he hadn't made a mistake. He gathered the cards again, tried, incoherently, to count to fifty-four, allowing for the two jokers in the deck. He tried to count around the table, to determine who was playing, who was sitting out a hand; there seemed to be an extra player in the game. But the basement was dark, the players slumped into their mutual grayness, their exhaustion. They said yes and no indifferently, they nodded and shook their heads at once. Liebhaber could hardly see beyond the deck of cards in his raised left hand.

"I can't stay," Straw said. He was trying to get up from the table. His coat snagged on a nail; he'd already torn the sleeve three times.

"Count the damned cards," somebody grumbled.

As weary as the men were, they understood the concern, the desperation of that voice. Possibly half of them pushed back the two benches, their blocks of wood, bent down to search on the dirt floor, under the table. Liebhaber picked up the candle at his elbow, carefully he lowered it down below the picnic table's edge.

The roar that went up that morning, into the still, frozen air over the town of Big Indian, was third only to Vera Lang's immortal cry and the cry that was to come from the air itself, many years later, over Big Indian.

Who first saw Martin Lang's two smashed legs, bent oddly away from the knees, the feet twisted out of their natural position, was never determined. Why all those stooped and spent men reacted in unison, at what signal they found their common fear and terror, remained a mystery. Who it was that burst away from the vision, knocked over the last blest and stolen candle, knocked all the players into blackest night, that too was never resolved.

At six o'clock in the morning, at the exact moment when Jerry Lapanne was scheduled to be, or to have been, hanged, the sleeping citizens of Big Indian heard so perverse an ululation that not one single sleeper rose from his bed to go to a window. Some citizens of the town, because of secession moves, claimed to be on Mountain Standard Time: they insisted the cry arose one hour too late to signify anything, for the penitentiary was in another time zone. Some citizens claimed to be on Mountain Daylight Time: they were willing to set their very watches by the saving of a life. One and all, they buried their heads under their blankets. They held their breath: for something more than a minute. They prayed, the listeners. They gripped their hands into their chilled crotches. They hugged each other, those who slept together. They were, all of them, too horrified to weep or to moan or to ask a single question. Children learned stillness. The old experienced the call of death, heard it, and welcomed the summons.

The roar was an animal roar. Some remembered it, after, as a bull sound, ferocious, out of the dark earth itself, the sound of the darkness itself. Some remembered the horses that drowned when Skandl's lighthouse broke through the ice, the lost and drowning team abandoned by all, trumpeting a perfection of despair. Some thought a pack of wolves was loosened on the town, purely and simply rabies mad, yelping and howling to a final feast.

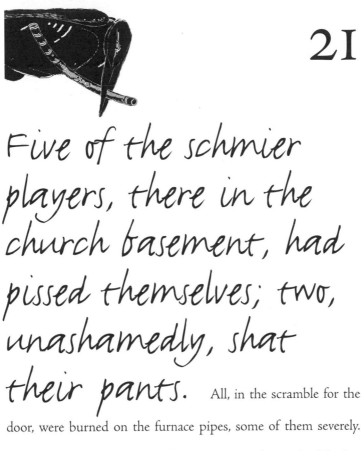

21

Five of the schmier players, there in the church basement, had pissed themselves; two, unashamedly, shat their pants. All, in the scramble for the door, were burned on the furnace pipes, some of them severely. Marvin Straw lost the seat of his trousers and considerable skin to the hot door of the furnace. Leo Weller, rescuing the deck of cards, drove splinters under three nails of his right hand, and had to dig them out with a jackknife. Andy Wolbeck lost the shoe of his artificial foot, and went partially barefoot into the street. The smell of urine and excrement — and, according to some observers, sulphur — hung in the streets of Big Indian through the entire day.

Emil Wind, the owner of the hotel, was at first delighted; by sundown of that day he'd sold more beer than had ever been sold in one week in the history of Big Indian. The card players were men totally without hope. Their condition was infectious: by eight o'clock in the evening, every white adult male in the municipality was hell-bent on getting blind drunk. For the first and only time ever, in the whole municipality, it was no disgrace to pass out in your chair in the beer parlor, to fall down dead drunk in the street. Men lay in their own vomit, gagging and crying. Husbands ignored the entreaties of their wives, fathers denied so much as a nickel or dime to the children waiting in parked cars, refused their own off-spring the consolation of an Oh Henry! bar or a bottle of Big Orange in the Chinaman's across the street. Wives and mothers, pleading at the door of the beer parlor, were jeered and mocked at.

Some people, later, claimed it was Vera Lang who summoned the RCMP; others tried to put the blame on Marvin Straw, even though he was in mortal pain, the blisters on his burned ass breaking, the dried puss glueing his spent body to the beer parlor chair. Whatever the case, the police from the nearest detachment, fifty miles away, arrived in full force; within an hour they were at their wits' end, in their attempts to deal with the chaos.

There were no cars to search, as on a dance night, for hidden mickeys and twenty-sixes and cases of beer. There were no women, as in a roadblock, to force out of a car, with the expectation that bottles of beer might cascade from beneath a carefully arranged skirt. There was nothing to confiscate, nothing to take home to their own parties. The despairing drinkers were barricaded in the beer parlor, beyond the reach of reason. It was futile to appeal to the common sense of the one man in town who wasn't in the rage and racket of the beer parlor: old Father Basil had rushed from the church basement up to the confession box and gone to confession himself. He was never again to set foot in the basement of his own church, and throughout the entire winter that was to follow, one of the coldest in living memory, he said Mass each Sunday in a church that froze the wine in the chalice each time he tried to take a ritual drink.

By 10:45 PM on the day the schmier players knocked down the door of the basement and escaped from the Church of the Final Virgin, every white male over the age of twenty in the Municipal District of Bigknife had been put on the Indian list; not one of them could, legally, be served an alcoholic beverage.

The dispossessed men, drunk, shouting, farting, whining, hollering, cursing, belching, swearing, puking, spitting, were forced out of the beer parlor, into the street. Some of them collapsed into the arms of waiting wives. Some of them crawled into cars and immediately fell asleep. Some of them, their joy turned to rage, began to fight in the streets, smashing senselessly at each other's bodies while still others cheered them on. There were thirteen minor car accidents in the vicinity of Big Indian in less than twenty-four minutes. One driver drove through his own garage wall and into the potato patch behind it. Another, unable to change gears, tried to back all the way home, and two miles south of town hit a dugout; fortunately the car was waterproof and floated until next morning. Another, mistaking the railway bridge for a hayrack, turned to avoid it and drove into the Bigknife River.

The schmier players, even when under pressure from the outraged police, did not panic. Leo Weller held them together, at the door of the lobby of the hotel, insisting they must be allowed back in to look for Liebhaber. He explained, loftily, that all men were equal before the law, that every man was innocent until proven guilty; the police responded by ordering the unruly players to stand with upraised arms against the brick wall of the old hotel.

Liebhaber had passed out in the can of the beer parlor. He was awakened by a constable whose first command was, "Get your hands out of there and pull up your pants." Liebhaber, held by the scruff of his neck while his exhausted fellow players not so much leaned against the wall as clung to its bricks, was in a state of total collapse.

"Gutenberg did this to me," he said.

The young mountie twisted Liebhaber's right arm up behind his back. "Let's have the truth," he said.

It came to him in that instant, the mountie twisting his arm, his friends in agony, leaning with their hands raised against the brick wall of the old hotel. Liebhaber knew it was Gutenberg who'd made all memory of the past irrelevant. His fly open, the mountie pulling his shirt tight around his neck, he understood: only the future, and that just barely, was free of Gutenberg's vast design.

And then, quietly, not intending in any way to resist, trying still to button his trousers with his free hand, Liebhaber startled himself with his own announcement:

"John Skandl is about to return to Big Indian. He is returning to the assistance of his beleaguered people. He will return by airplane."

The astounded card players, their arms aching so they could hardly flex a finger, gave all together a grunt and a squeal of delight. "We're saved," Leo Weller said, dropping his left hand to the U stamped on his forehead, the police be damned. "Yi-peeeee," Eddie Brausen shouted; he raised the missing finger of his raised left hand in defiance of the law. Art Van Slyke let down his arms and smashed his nose against the wall; he broke his nose. Up until that moment, there hadn't been a thing in the world wrong with him. They needed no further instructions, those spent, hungover men. They fled from the wall, ignoring the shouted commands of the confused RCMP. They stumbled and fell from the sidewalk, out into the rutted gravel street. They headed down the street, turned in a ragged column into a dark alley; they were following Liebhaber now, following his memory of the future. John Skandl was returning to the assistance of his beleaguered people. They listened for the plane.

22

They walked down to the riverbank. They found Skandl's old granary where it had been left, years earlier; they knocked the padlock off the door. Nesting swallows and sparrows, over the years, had covered the floor with mud and grass and droppings. Skandl's lantern, as if by a miracle, still contained coal oil. The hungover men kicked some of the debris out the door as best they could. They scavenged for boards with which to enlarge the table. They found some cardboard and a gunnysack and made a stab at patching the broken panes in the window that Skandl had used as his toilet.

Scrounging through their pockets, they came up with enough money to send young Eddie Brausen to the bootlegger for two cases of beer. He was back in half an hour with the sad news that the bootlegger himself was ready to pay any price for a drink. Some of the men groaned, threatening to fall back into despair. But now it was Marvin Straw who dealt with the crisis: "Things are adding up," he said. He sent three men to steal potatoes from the nearest potato patch.

By dawn, Straw had a batch of potato champagne cooking on the oil-drum stove. The players sat down, relaxed and confident, to a hand of schmier. The previous dawn was forgotten or ignored. Skandl would arrive soon. He'd be the richest and rashest player ever. Their finely honed card skills would make them all winners. They played with a new vigor, the twelve men, and even when Skandl had not arrived by sundown, as they'd expected he might, since he was flying, their faith in Liebhaber's memory of the future was undaunted. Nor did the next day's disappointment dampen their spirits; Liebhaber himself was only spurred on to a more absolute conviction by the temporary failure of his pronouncement to prove true.

Joe Lightning was the first visitor to challenge, directly, the players' new belief in future. He and Cathy had moved out of their car body for the winter and had gone to a log cabin on the reserve. They'd been there nearly a month before Joe listened to the entreaties of his mother-in-law and went to try and reason with the players.

"For Christ's sake, quit," Joe said, through the open window of the granary; he couldn't stand the smell inside.

"Keep your voice down," Straw said, "we're listening for an airplane." Liebhaber no longer deigned to argue with anyone. Marvin Straw was acting as his spokesman: "John Skandl will be here any minute."

"So will the second coming," Joe said. He'd become, just before his wedding, Shuffleboard Champion of the Great Plains, and he no longer minced words.

"Bugger off," Straw said. Sometimes he still felt the natural authority of a man who had hanged offenders against the law.

"Booze," Joe Lightning countered. He was trying to be reasonable. "Maybe the cops'd take the heat off you guys if you'd stop drinking and gambling."

"Skandl will want to play a game or two," Straw said.

"Women," Joe Lightning argued, almost sticking his head in at the broken window. "Without booze, the women aren't getting laid. They're up at the reserve half the time, pretending to buy fenceposts or blueberries. Their men can't screw when they're sober."

Joe himself had set up in business cutting fenceposts, and was doing it seriously. But he knew that a lot of the men on the reserve were using that occupation as a front, so they might entertain horny women from in and around Big Indian. The town had been named after a little Cree trapper who could sweep eight quarters off a beer table with one swing of his hammer. The Indian males over twenty were now the only people in the Municipal District of Bigknife who were allowed to purchase alcoholic beverages.

"Let me deal you in," Straw suggested.

Joe Lightning left in disgust. It was the first time ever that a sane, adult male had refused to join the game. Liebhaber felt it was an ill omen. "Damn drunk Indians," he said.

That same exchange, years later, would lead the two men to become friends. Liebhaber, at the time, had dropped out of the game on 128 occasions. The players were paying each other with matches someone had found in Skandl's cupboard.

The matches gave out, a week later, because some of the men were trying to smoke a mixture of rope and dried rhubarb leaves and a sprinkling of horse shit rolled in brown wrapping paper. Bill Morgan suggested they try notched sticks and split willows but the process of forever running outside to cut more willows interfered with the game. Alphonse Martz went to the nearest general store and stole a box of toothpicks. The players used up the toothpicks in one hour after trying to eat a boiled skunk they'd killed when it took refuge under the granary. Liebhaber, a day or two later, lost the entire pile of clam shells that he'd picked up along the banks of the freezing river. He slammed down his fist on the ace, deuce and ten of diamonds and quit the game; he'd got as far as Main Street, was turning the corner toward the hotel, before he remembered he was on the Indian list.

It was the ninth batch of Marvin Straw's home brew that led Liebhaber to come up with a suggestion. He hated to criticize his spokesman, but this was beyond endurance. "We can no longer sit like a bunch of dummies, twiddling our thumbs. We must contact Mr. Skandl at once and insist that he go through with his secession scheme before he flies here to join us in a few hands of schmier." Someone complained bitterly of farting blue flames. "Get some decent liquor laws on the books," Liebhaber explained. He took another swig from the jug.

"Which province are we in now?" Heck asked.

No one could answer with any certainty.

Obviously, they had to send someone in search of Skandl, someone who could reason with him, explain that it was essential for the municipality to secede immediately. Bill Morgan, wiping at his empty eye socket, blinking, thought they should forget about Saskatchewan and join Alberta. Droniuk wondered if they hadn't done that by plebiscite, at the last election, whenever that was. Eddie Brausen, young and still optimistic, raising his missing finger at the world, felt they should forget both provinces and join a wet American state. Leo Weller said they must send out a messenger, an emissary, to explain the immediate predicament to Skandl. He was on his way, but he was taking his time.

Mick O'Holleran hated arguments. He suggested they play cards to settle the issue.

That game began at midnight on December 16. The rules were simple enough: they would play until one man had all the real money. The winner must use it to leave Big Indian and travel in search of John Skandl.

The battle went on for six hours, some of the men desperate to win, desperate to leave the game, the granary, the town itself. Then, unexpectedly, Isador Heck, three times in a row, was dealt the ace, the three spot, the jack and the ten: Isador Heck, who didn't believe in the existence of a world beyond the Municipal District of Bigknife. He couldn't resist bidding four on such a near-perfect hand. Three times in a row, he caught the king and queen with his ace, saved the jack, took home the game. Three times in a row his three stood up for low.

Andy Wolbeck gave Heck a pass to ride on the CNR. He departed with eighteen dollars, persuaded even as he stepped up off the little bench and into the passenger car of the morning train that the place he was bound for could only be an illusion.

23

The remaining players, painfully aware that their number had been diminished by one, had hardly

dealt a new hand when Vera Lang drove up to the granary door. At first they thought they heard an airplane; every last player dropped his cards and rushed away from the table. Vera drove right up to the door in Skandl's old Essex.

She had on, along with her usual winter clothes, a bee veil She'd taken to covering her entire body. "John Skandl is missing," she said, speaking through the veil.

"We know," Marvin Straw said. He was standing in the midst of the ragged bodies; as usual, he was speaking for Liebhaber. The other players, finding their hands free, began to scratch. Straw was holding a handful of shingle nails. "Isador's gone to find him. He'll be right back."

Vera shook her head. "He was flying. He was coming here in a Piper Cub, intending to land in our pasture. The plane disappeared."

"He'll make it," Marvin Straw insisted, polite, undoubting. He had come to a hard confidence in his role as mouthpiece; he was in charge of the very nails they used now paying each other.

"He's missing," Vera said. She explained softly, but firmly too, an edge in her voice that was almost an edge of desire. "He's *missing*."

The silence was broken only when Liebhaber burst out: "How would you know? How would you know, then, if he didn't get here; how would you know he didn't get here?" He groped for a corner of his mustache and found his face matted in hair. He scratched. "It's a rumor. A dirty·lie. It's a trap to make us surrender."

"Surrender?" Vera said. "Surrender *what?*"

"The world," Liebhaber shouted. "The world…" He was confused. He scratched at himself with both hands. "It's a scab and a carbuncle. A bucket of medicated puke. A horse turd everlastingly falling…"

"Mother sent him the money to rent the plane. He phoned for money. He felt he should come back in style."

She was leaving. Vera was turning away to leave. Liebhaber and half the other men stepped down from the granary's doorway. Leo Weller, his shoes worn out, stepped in his stocking feet, his toes and heels naked, into the fresh snow. Art Van Slyke, hopping out of the granary, slipped and fell, smashed his broken and infected nose against the end of a skid. He was unsteady from ten days of diarrhea. Nick Droniuk stopped dead in the doorway; he hadn't looked up at the sky in a week. The light blinded him. They had, all of them, long ago, refused to give any credence to the weather, especially to the idea of seasons.

Vera opened the door of her Essex. She hesitated, one foot on the running board. "Mother's been supporting him. Every year. If it wasn't for my bees…"

Vera Lang raised her veil. She lifted the veil, to utter whatever imprecation it was she intended.

In that single instant, Marvin Straw fell hopelessly in love.

Vera almost let herself smile. "Men are a bunch of useless bastards." She disappeared into her car, slammed shut the door.

Marvin Straw had seen in a glance the perfect beauty of Vera Lang's face. He, alone, of all those men, had not heard the outcry on the afternoon of her seduction by the swarming bees. Had he heard the call, had he been told the story, he might have saved himself. One telling of the story might have saved him. He saw only the perfect beauty of her face, polished as bright and smooth as beeswax. He had been given no warning. In the glacial blue of her scornful eyes, he read a summons out through the gates; he read, and did not for a moment understand, a promise of painful bliss. She wrote her face upon his sorrow. He gave an inarticulate groan. The devastation of love was his.

Marvin Straw, at the instant when he might have saved himself with a single resolve, stepped away from the granary. Like a crazy dog he leapt, galloped, yapped in pursuit of the vanishing automobile.

24

On the night of December 18, in the valley of the Bigknife River, the mercury hit fifty-eight degrees below zero, Fahrenheit.

Tiddy, at dawn, went out to the barn and found that the milk cow nearest the door had frozen teats. She thought of the men huddled around their card table in John Skandl's flimsy granary. The game, since its beginning on a Sunday morning in her kitchen, had been in progress for 151 days. She harnessed her old black mare. She built a fire in the small stove in her new closed-in cutter.

The poplars along the road were swollen with hoarfrost; the telephone lines and the barbed wires of the fences, pulled taut by the iron cold, were thickened with crystals of ice. Columns of smoke stood straight up over the chimneys of Big Indian, pillars giving support to a frozen sky. Tiddy, looking down into the valley, thought of the frost, blooming white on the heads of nails in the shrinking granary. No one cut ice now, on the river; the river itself was abandoned to the cold. She urged her frost-whitened horse down the long road into the coulee. The planks on the deck of the bridge rang hollow. Ice fog blurred Main Street.

The eleven remaining players were more corpses than men. They hardly stirred, hardly looked up from their cards, when the door squeaked open on its frosted hinges. Tiddy beheld the spectres of the men she had once fed, even fattened. They'd suffered frostbite, in the earlier days of winter, one of the coldest on record; the feet of some of the men smelled of rotting skin and gangrene. They'd tried cooking an old set of harness and the smell of boiled leather and sweat and horse shit mingled with that of dead flesh and dirty socks. Earlier, they'd cooked dogs and cats; then, when the people of the town began to protect their pets, they'd taken to breaking into muskrat houses, to setting snares for disease-weakened rabbits. They knew now where to find garbage cans before the garbage was picked up on a cold morning, how to dig through the nuisance grounds, how to steal firewood from a woodpile; they had once caught a magpie in a gopher trap and devoured it, fried in a batter made from the oats they'd scraped up off the ground where boxcars were being loaded beside a grain elevator.

Tiddy asked them to come to her house.

"No," Liebhaber said. He was ahead in the game, about to win a few nails and some pieces of broken glass and a pile of round stones they'd dug up from the frozen riverbed with their bare hands. "Never."

"Some homemade bread. Fresh out of the oven. With homemade butter and homemade apricot jam."

Liebhaber was holding high in the air the king of clubs, ready to slap it down. He noticed, for the first time in weeks, the filthiness of his hands; they were shit-brown. He tried to conceal them from Tiddy.

"Some fresh pancakes. With warmed-up chokecherry jelly."

Liebhaber slammed down the king. "No."

"Fresh eggs." Tiddy could hardly stand the smell in the crowded room; she backed toward the open door, finding an excuse to cup a hand to her nose. "A quart of sausage. Some raw-fried potatoes with onion…"

Leo Weller put the ace on Liebhaber's king.

"Coffee," Tiddy said. She was calling, now, from the doorway. "Fresh cream, so thick you can serve it with a spoon."

"Schmier," Droniuk said. He simply couldn't stand it. He put the ten spot on Leo Weller's ace. He wanted to quit. He wanted to go home. He sacrificed a point, playing against Liebhaber's bid.

"Schmier," Eddie Brausen said. He was too young. He remembered a clean bed, and the splash of water on his face in the morning, and a warm kitchen smelling of homemade bread; he remembered the color of whole strawberries in a tin of strawberry jam, and the laughter of women and children, and the sound of a fiddle being tuned. Eddie Brausen played the jack, gave the jack to Leo Weller. He wanted to lose everything; he wanted to get out.

Liebhaber was set. He had another hickey. "The world," he shouted, "is a pimple on an alligator's ass. The world is a rotten fish, a broken hamestrap, a tub of shit." He slammed down his queen on the bare table; his frost-stiffened fingers nearly broke. "No," he shouted. "Never. No. Not now. Not ever. Never. No. Never. No. Never. Not ever. No."

Tiddy hesitated at the door. "Vera has some honey in the comb."

It was then that Marvin Straw finally spoke up. He was lying ill on the cot in a corner of the granary. The effect of his single glimpse of Vera Lang had never left him. He began to beg, hoarsely:

"Please, God, let us go to Tiddy's house, wherever that is. I'm starving. I'm freezing. I'm perishing sick, and dying of my own misery. If we can't go to Tiddy's house, then hang me instead. Then stab me while I'm hanging. Then shoot me while I'm bleeding to death."

They walked the mile through the bitter cold, the men, all of them refusing a ride in Tiddy's cutter. The out-of-doors was somehow warmer than the granary. They walked in a straggling file across the ice, Liebhaber bringing up the rear, Marvin Straw, for all his illness, in the lead; slowly, in pain, they climbed, helping each other feebly up the coulee bank, up the hill. They walked past the big poplar at the foot of the garden, its branches bare to the ferocious cold. They walked under the clothesline wires where the figure of Martin Lang, on stormy days, on moonlit nights, plowed the snow. They trailed in a single, exhausted column through the gate, stumbled up the three steps, crossed the porch.

The table was set. Tiddy had beaten the men to the house, driving around by the road. Tiddy's daughters had seen the men coming up the valley: they had sliced long strips off a slab of smoked bacon. They were frying eggs and pancakes. It was Rose, not Vera, who broke the honey-filled combs into a dish; it was Anna Marie who toasted thick slices of homemade bread in a wire rack on top of the stove.

Old Lady Lang was pouring coffee from the huge pot that was used during threshing time. She poured the rich, steaming coffee into cups set in a row beside the cream pitcher; the aroma seemed to lift the frost from the frozen cheeks of the gasping and puffing men.

The black crow watched Liebhaber pull off the rags that had once been a camel-pile coat. "Well, Leeb," it said, "I've got to hand it to you. You are finally a total asshole."

"Listen, crow, go fuck yourself with a wire brush," Liebhaber said; that same Liebhaber who for days and nights had defended the black crow against its critics. Liebhaber, for the first time in 151 days, lost complete control of his temper. "Crow," he went on, "you are a little turd. A teeny-weeny turd. You are a prick with ears."

"Gentlemen," the crow said, ignoring the insults, "I want to welcome you back. We missed your filthy mouths and your slovenly behavior. We missed your abrasive laziness and your dirt and your stink. May you all die abnormal deaths."

JG, locked up in the parlor, hearing the men return, was excited beyond all reason; but he couldn't speak a sound. He farted loudly out of pure joy.

"I'm a happy man," Liebhaber said, defiantly to the crow. "I've decided to live forever."

The crow laughed whatever it was that passed for a laugh with a crow. It gagged and croaked and sort of bounced up and down. It had more to say, obviously; it had prepared a whole speech for the occasion of the cardplayers' return.

But it was Marvin Straw who got all the attention. His infatuation with Vera Lang had wrecked his mind. She was seated at one end of the kitchen table, reading a new issue of a journal on beekeeping, rubbing at her face with a damp cloth, hardly deigning to notice the intruders. Marvin was hopelessly in love; he groaned and muttered. It was because of him and his infatuation that Liebhaber was able, unnoticed, to deal the first hand of schmier, right there at Tiddy's dining room table, with only Leo Weller showing the slightest interest in the game. Rita Lang, writing a letter at the far end of the table, ignored him completely. O'Holleran was catching all hell from Rose, somewhere in an upstairs bedroom; everyone could hear her scolding. Droniuk had disappeared into a bedroom with his wife, Anna Marie; she'd left her comb on the kitchen table.

Liebhaber was dealing when the phone rang.

Tiddy, during the schmier game, had had a phone installed. Without Liebhaber's visits, with no men visiting, she'd had to subscribe to the party line. Her ring was four shorts and a long; no one failed to rubber when her number was called.

The phone rang, the four shorts and a long in quick succession. It was central calling.

"Hello," Tiddy said. The phone was in the dining room, just inside the door from the kitchen. Tiddy, at that instant, noticed that Liebhaber was dealing. He looked up from the cards, saw her head of thick red hair, her fierce blue eyes, her skin that was immune to all weather.

"Hello," the black crow said. With a quick hop it was in the parlor with JG. The black crow hated the phone. The phone had ruined all its pleasures.

"Found?" Tiddy said. She sounded dumbstruck.

"Found?" the black crow mocked.

"*Found?*" Tiddy insisted. Demanded.

She was silent, listening. Then, instead of speaking, she nodded her head. Then she staggered into the kitchen, almost fell into a chair at the kitchen table.

Vera Lang put down her new journal on top of her worn copy of Root's ABC *and* XYZ *of Bee Culture*, squared one on top of the other. She went, carefully, into the dining room, refusing to notice either Liebhaber or Leo Weller at the dining room table.

"Yes?" she said.

"___"

"Yes."

"___"

"We'll be right there."

"___"

"Yes."

"___"

"Yes."

"___"

"I said we'll be right there."

Liebhaber, at that exact moment, formulated his intention of winning immortality by becoming a philosopher. He would ask himself the single question: "Why do human beings wake up in the morning?" Yes; he would ask, and reconsider, and answer too: why would any person, having been fortunate enough to fall asleep, wake up? It was a question that would occupy his thoughts many times in the years to come. At that exact moment he thought the answer might be simply another question: might not death, too, one day, get sick of everything and die?

Vera Lang hung up the receiver and went into the kitchen and sat down at the kitchen table. Leo Weller followed her. The black crow followed, too, lighting on the back of the empty high chair.

Mick and Rose O'Holleran came downstairs; Rose was carrying in a small shoe box the fragments of a mirror she'd just then broken, earning seven years of bad luck; at least she'd give it a decent burial. Nick and Anna Marie Droniuk came down the stairs behind them; Anna Marie's long black hair, for the first time in her life, was a mess. Andy Wolbeck, watching, pulled off a dirty sock and fingered his ivory toes. Cruickshank, brushing the hair out of his own eyes, got honey in his hair, got honey in his beard. Art Van Slyke dipped a piece of toast into the yolk of a fried egg, then missed his mouth; his swollen nose distorted his vision. Eddie Brausen was at the sink, trying to wash his face. He'd forgotten how. He pulled at the towel on the roller, looking for a dry spot. He gave up, wiped the backs of his hands on the legs of his trousers, and went to find a chair. Marvin Straw stared at Vera Lang.

Liebhaber was last to join the group at the kitchen table. He was carrying a worn-out deck of cards. Only Rita was absent. She was listening from the next room, writing a letter.

"John Skandl is dead," Vera Lang said. She was looking at her hands to make certain they were clean. "My son found him."

"Your son?" Liebhaber said. He put down the deck of cards on the kitchen table.

"My son," Vera said. Dispassionately. She might have been preparing the district news for a page in the *Big Indian Signal*. "Vera's Boy."

"Your *son?*" two people demanded at once, possibly three: Leo Weller and Rose O'Holleran, and possibly Ken Cruickshank.

"You mean your *son* is alive?" more people chimed in. Anna Marie Droniuk reached for her comb. Mick O'Holleran, in violent reluctance to believe his own ears, stamped his missing foot. Andy Wolbeck, accidentally, twisted off one of his artificial toes.

25

"Coyotes," Vera said. She wiped, fastidiously, at the corners of her mouth with a paper serviette, though she had not yet taken a bite of any of the food heaped on the table. "He's living with a den of coyotes, it would appear. It was he who signaled to the search party." She turned condescendingly to Liebhaber. "My son located the crashed plane that no one else could find, the frozen corpse..."

The card players scrambled up from the table. Whether they intended to flee or to search was not clear. Perhaps they recalled their encounter with Martin Lang, and were undecided. They raced to put on boots, to don the tattered remnants of sweaters and coats and caps. They were shouting for details; they demanded details of Vera, of Tiddy, of each other. They were at the phone again, ringing a confusing series of rings, scaring poor JG half out of his wits: soft, ripe excrement trickled down his left pantleg onto the parlor floor.

Vera, alone at the kitchen table, poured herself a cup of coffee. She moved the bread and butter and the dish of honey to where she might comfortably reach them; she found a clean knife. It was not she but rather Tiddy who picked up the filthy deck of cards. Tiddy took the cards to the stove, lifted a lid with a poker. She dropped Liebhaber's deck of cards into the flames and put down the lid on the puff of stinking smoke.

Rose O'Holleran sighed. She'd left a lot of the chores undone. She'd hoped that the men, finally, after so many months, would do the chores.

Three children came down the stairs. They'd been sitting on the top step of the stairs, quiet together, secretly listening. "Can we eat now?" Theresa O'Holleran asked. She was already picking at the bacon dish, trying to find a strip that was crisp to her liking.

Old Lady Lang reached into her apron pocket, carefully fondled her ball of sorrow. She was sitting on the woodbox, beside the stove; the door was open so much of the time, she was having trouble keeping warm. "It's too sad," she said. To no one. "I don't want to think about it."

26

Ice forming on the wings of the Piper Cub had caused the crash:

that was easy enough to determine. But no one recognized at the
time that a war was breaking out between the sky and the earth.
Hostilities were intensifying, but no one noticed because all the
attention was focused on Vera's Boy. He arrived at the farm in the
back of the same pickup truck that carried the corpse of John
Skandl. He was squatting down in the straw wearing moccasins
and trousers and a shirt and rough parka, all his clothing made of
the gunnysacks that farmers left in their fields during harvest.
Vera's Boy was neat and clean enough, except for a tendency to
wipe his runny nose with his hair. What astonished people was
the way he jabbered on, hardly stopping to listen, in a kind of
speech that was half yips and barks, half what his listeners took to
be pig Latin.

When the truck pulled up to the kitchen door, Vera took her son by the hand and led him into the kitchen. Tiddy insisted that the huge, frozen corpse be carried through the house to the bedroom, to her bed, where it might be thawed out and washed and properly dressed before the undertaker saw it. Father Basil arrived at the farm while Old Lady Lang and Rose, with dishrags and the blue graniteware basin full of soapy water, were bathing the body. The old priest asked that a few of the men decide at once when they'd dig the grave. They said they'd do it first thing in the morning. Vera's Boy, squatting on a chair by the kitchen table — and he was never to learn to sit — eating an ice-cream cone, interrupted the priest to say, in his buzzing way, "Erellthay be nowsay in the orningmay."

That was the first hint anyone had of his ability to sense the forthcoming weather. No one, at the time, guessed that the boy's simple talent was to be the basis of the next wave of prosperity in the Municipal District of Bigknife. Rather, Tiddy, coming out of the bedroom to get the towel that was warming on the back of a chair by the stove, was somewhat embarrassed at the boy's bad manners and said so to Vera. Not until next morning, when four of the ex-cardplayers went to dig the grave in the graveyard behind the church and almost got lost in a snow squall, did anyone recognize the implications of the boy's statement.

John Skandl's wake was one of the finest ever held in the district. He'd been hauled out of the coulee in the box of a half-ton that was full of straw — someone had taken the trouble to cut the strings on two bales while the body was being lifted out of the wrecked Piper Cub — and Vera, trying to sweep up under everyone's feet, was furious at finding bits of straw from one end of the house to the other. Some animal — perhaps a lynx or a weasel, living in the coulee where the plane went down — had got at Skandl before Vera's Boy, up on the edge of the valley, signaled to a search party. Curiously, the dead man was laid out flat in the wrecked plane. The searchers saw a body that most of the guests at the wake were never to see, for the casket had to be kept closed. Only late in the second night did two of the ex-cardplayers, Bill Morgan and Alphonse Martz, sitting up with the corpse and a case of beer, venture to take a peek. Skandl looked silly without ears. Shocked at the spectacle, they hid two bottles of beer in the coffin.

All the reformed players, spic and span, dressed in brand-new clothes, shaved and barbered, patched and bandaged, showed up for the funeral. The church smelled of Rawleigh's Medicated Ointment. Tiddy, dressed in black and wearing a veil, conducted herself with decorum and asked the priest to keep the sermon modest and brief. He did so in church. Unfortunately, while standing at the graveside in the falling snow, with Mr. Aardt waiting to let go of his hernia and lower the coffin, he was struck by a new theory of evolution.

"My dear friends," he intoned, signaling the altar boy to pass the holy water. "It strikes me..." He raised his right hand to sprinkle holy water into the grave. "We come from life, we pass into..."

The water was frozen in the sprinkler.

Father Basil gave the sprinkler another shake. "Hold it under your arm," he said to the bare-headed, shivering boy at his right.

In the next eighty minutes, the boy desperately clutching the sprinkler in his left armpit, Father Basil developed his theory that all inanimate matter evolved out of animate matter, witness the case of John Skandl himself. He extended the comparison to the nearest visible galaxies and looked forward to the ideal condition of total inanimateness for the entire universe.

The widow was about to collapse. Liebhaber, standing at her side, gently took her arm. Father Basil stood outlined against the bleak prairie sky. The fence behind him, intended to keep cows from grazing in the graveyard, was in places completely drifted over with snow.

"Now we can get married," Liebhaber whispered in Tiddy's ear, "and give our son a father."

"Every rock and stone and chip," Father Basil was venturing, "every moon and meteorite — with the possible exception of comets — was once living matter. The universe was alive to its own breathing. Each planet and star is only a cell in the body which we, in our small blindness, cannot conceive." He lifted his cold hands against the tumble and fall of snow.

"We could get married," Liebhaber whispered. He was shaking with the cold, inside his new parka.

"Men live, men die," Father Basil said. "And that is the truth of it."

"Please," Liebhaber pleaded. "I'll never play schmier again. I promise."

Snow was falling, the light was thin. Liebhaber felt again on his back the clinging, dead figure of Martin Lang. He was weighted down, into the frozen earth.

Liebhaber was approaching despair. He held Tiddy's elbow, the firm clean line of her elbow, under the black sleeve, in his stiff hand. Liebhaber, for all the world's dying, in love.

Tiddy turned. She put her warm mouth to Liebhaber's ear. He was no taller than she. His head went dizzy. She moved her mouth close, the warmth of her breath a balm on his freezing ear. She whispered into his cocked ear: "I must go into mourning, Gus." She was moved to tears. She was moved to an eloquence of her own, by Father Basil's eloquent confounding of the mereness of an end: she would weep. "I have to go into mourning. Now. For two years, Gus; one would never be sufficient."

27

While Tiddy wore a black crepe band on the left sleeve of her coat,

the rest of the municipality began to rejoice: the genius of Vera's Boy for understanding weather had become apparent. He could walk into the corner of a tilled field and sense on his skin the moisture conditions, and then, with his blue eyes shut under his black eyebrows, announce what crop would best thrive that season. He could, with a single sniff of the air, recognize the ideal seeding time while the local forecasters scratched in the cold soil and licked their fingers and tested the wind in vain. He could predict a sunny day for a baseball tournament; he could tell a farmer when to cut hay or not to cut hay; he could guess when the frost would come and advise the harvesters when to start cutting. The only and minor difficulty was that he spoke, always, a language that no one quite understood. There was, sometimes, a kind of buzz in his breathing; the kinder neighbors, hearing the sound, suggested he'd contracted asthma, while living in the coyote's den. And he had become, in a matter of months, something of dandy in his dress, liking especially anything made of leather.

The strange thing was, though, he had no need of women. It was true that on occasion, especially when the moon was full, he would disappear for a night, return at dawn looking exhausted, spent. But he was as free of desire as Liebhaber was obsessed by it, and that was the first reason for Liebhaber's growing dislike.

Everyone else had nothing but praise for Vera's Boy. At the age of thirteen, within a year of his return, he was acclaimed the new reeve of the municipality. His wisdom brought with it such a pitch of prosperity, such a rejoicing in wheat and oats and cattle and hogs, that Father Basil finally preached his famous sermon on greed, for four hours and twenty minutes, to a completely deserted church. It was a clear, warm day in late fall, and everyone chose to spend that Sunday harvesting. The threshing crews got double pay. The women, cooking for the threshers, made Sunday dinner, then supper too, into a feast.

Tiddy had been mourning for two years and then some when Vera's Boy made his first miscalculation. He told Droniuk how to raise a half-section of perfect wheat. Fall came, the wheat stood waist high and yellow in the field. Everyone had forgotten about the sky's hostility. Nick Droniuk had won a prize as the best farmer in the district; he aspired to become wheat champion of the world.

He fell into his threshing machine while raging at the sky because the huge field of wheat proved to be all straw without grain. His testicles were blown into the granary, the rest of his body into the strawpile. His widow, Anna Marie, added the precious remains to the collection of aphrodisiacs she kept in her hope chest; she couched them on the wing of a mallard and wrapped them in a tanned rabbit skin. Liebhaber's secret joy at

Vera's Boy's miscalculation was annihilated when Tiddy decided, on the day of the Mass for the repose of Nick Droniuk's soul, to mourn now for her son-in-law.

Anna Marie and her three daughters moved into the Lang house and that too made Liebhaber's life more difficult. He had trusted to Tiddy's loneliness. O'Holleran and Droniuk both, in their first prosperity, had bought trailer homes and mounted them on cinder blocks and banked them with manure and added porches. But hardly were Nick Droniuk's remains collected and confided to the earth when Anna Marie returned to her mother's house. Rita was there too, but she was silent, seated at the dining room table, forever writing letters. Vera had moved from her upstairs room into the attic; and further, she was gone most of the day, visiting her bee yards, avoiding her insane suitor.

Marvin Straw had been driven crazy by his love for Vera Lang. He had gone stark, raving mad. He slept in ditches, in culverts, in patches of silver willow by prairie trails, in the clover planted beside a newly graded road, in the willows under a bridge. He lived anywhere along any path or road or trail where Vera might pass in her everlasting concern for her bees. Sometimes he'd call down from an old poplar or the roof of a deserted house to a passerby: "Things are adding up." But usually he was silent, the fever of love burning in his dirt-rimmed eyes. And Vera, inevitably, would drive on, repulsed by the filthy, haggard scarecrow that hung in the crotch of a poplar tree, that cowered behind the girder of a bridge, that lurked, knee-deep in a slough, in a stand of cattails, the wild hair wreathed in a cloud of dragonflies.

Liebhaber, watching the folly of Marvin Straw, was almost apprehensive as Tiddy's second period of mourning approached its end. He almost saw it as a stroke of good fortune when Gladys Wurtz's husband was killed.

Eli the Hutterite, as he came to be called in people's memories, was hit by a train. Contrary to Vera's Boy's predictions — and it was his second failure — the prairie thunder showers had for a whole season missed the Bigknife Hutterite Colony. Eli, driving into town to sell a load of geese that no longer had either enough to eat or a place to swim, noticed a cloud in the sky and slammed on the truck's brakes. He and the geese chanced to be on a railway track. A wheat train chanced to be coming around the bend.

Tiddy, this time, plunged into mourning with Father Basil's full approval. He hit on the notion that mourning was a legitimate form of birth control: the only way to keep men from dying was to keep them from being born. Hardly had Liebhaber heard the news — he began to make preparations to leave Big Indian forever — when Isador Heck returned.

Heck, when asked about the world beyond the municipality, would start to answer then he'd say, "It would make a pig laugh," and he'd burst into uncontrollable laughter. When finally he got control of his laughter, he sometimes told, in the beer parlor, of airplanes that flew without propellers, of highways that were made of solid cement but soared through the air. Then everyone else in the beer parlor broke into uncontrollable laughter.

Isador Heck had toured the continent as a man being shot from a cannon. It was the only job he could get, given his qualifications as a prairie wheat farmer. In his overview, in his looking down, he had seen vast patterns of streets, acres of parked cars, rows of identical houses, square blocks of banks and clip joints, the gaudy lights of amusement arcades, the dark windows of churches, columns of school children and soldiers, crowded graveyards — and the vision had corrected his misconceived notion that nothing existed. On the contrary, it struck him clearly, everything existed. Flying through the air, lifted away from the earth, looking down, he had, if nothing else, glimpsed that truth. Returned to solid ground, he could only reply to the ignorance around him, "It would make a pig laugh."

Liebhaber, looking at the man who had seen the world, listening to the laughter, was reminded that Heck had departed from the schmier game with every last cent of the other players' cash. It was obvious, the lesson: money would buy happiness.

Liebhaber, briefly, went into politics. He ran for reeve against Vera's Boy on the simple motto: No one will ever have to work again. His entire campaign was conducted through the *Big Indian Signal*; indeed, it was part of his strategy never to make a public appearance. Almost without effort he persuaded half the men in the district to put their money into penny stocks; once they'd made their fortunes, the entire community would benefit. Secession would never again be necessary.

Tiddy, at this time, had nearly completed her third period of mourning, and Liebhaber was counting the days. He had conceived, to his immense satisfaction, a perfect political state, a confederation, as he liked to put it, of mind and body and spirit. There'd been a bit of a dry spell, the country was starting to need rain. His scheme began to look necessary as well as plausible. It was the weather itself, along with Liebhaber's persuasive arguments, that led Mick O'Holleran to put his life savings into an oil drilling venture in the valley of the Bigknife River.

O'Holleran couldn't contain his delight at the thought of never having to work another day of his life. One afternoon he persuaded Vera Lang to give him a lift down into the valley, out onto the alkali flat where the drilling was in progress. Vera was going in her old Essex to check an apiary in a bend of the river. O'Holleran had noticed some unusual activity around the rig; he managed, in all the hustle and bustle, to climb up the derrick, intending to take a look for himself. The derrick man in the crow's nest shouted that it was a dry hole; they were pulling the drill column in preparation to leave.

O'Holleran, excited and outraged, realizing he'd once again lost every cent of his savings, intending to cast a glance up at the sky, looked directly into the sun. At the same time, he went to step on his leg that wasn't there.

Mick O'Holleran had lost his faith in himself. And it was not he alone who had come to doubt; the whole community was showing symptoms of a faint but uneasy skepticism. He fell, landing headfirst in an open bag of drilling mud. He gagged and choked in the fine gray powder. Like a chicken bathing in dust, he disappeared into a cloud of his own making. A single glass of water, had it been available, might have rescued him. Gasping, his throat thick, his eyes pure white and bulging in his dust-gray face, bursting his lungs at last, he threshed his way into a terrible drowning.

Liebhaber and Vera's Boy arrived at the scene within minutes of each other. They'd hardly had time to shake hands before another car arrived. Tiddy was first to get out of the back seat. She was followed by the widow, Rose; Rose, in turn, was followed by her older daughter, Theresa.

Tiddy saw the two politicians standing together at the base of the derrick and cried out at once to both of them: "I'm going to mourn until there's a cloudburst."

Vera's Boy had no interest at all in the suffering of women. He had something of his mother's distance about him, something bordering on contempt for the merely human, and especially disliked fits of emotion.

"The ercilessmay unsay shall urnbay us," he yipped and barked. "Be reparedpay."

Tiddy turned to Liebhaber. He was staring up at the rig, at the derrick and the lengths of steel that pointed into the empty sky.

Liebhaber was about to declare his innocence, he was about to refuse responsibility for anything that happened anywhere in the world, O'Holleran be damned, Isador Heck be damned, widows and children be damned, profit and loss be damned, life be lamented and damned, death be kicked in the ass and damned, Vera and her bees be damned, the lonesome ghost of Martin Lang be damned, Tiddy herself be nothing but damned, when he remembered, for the third time in his life, the future.

Liebhaber, staring up at the derrick, at the empty prairie sky, standing there on the alkali flat, the sun and the wind-lifted alkali dust and the pain of his own seeing burning his eyes; Gus Liebhaber, his hands in his pockets, imagining for himself a woman, not expecting to speak a single word of what he was thinking or feeling, abruptly announced to the roughnecks and to the bereaved family and to the gathering crowd:

"We're going to be afflicted with a flood. That's the one certainty we have in our miserable lives. We're going to have one godawful nut-buster of a flood."

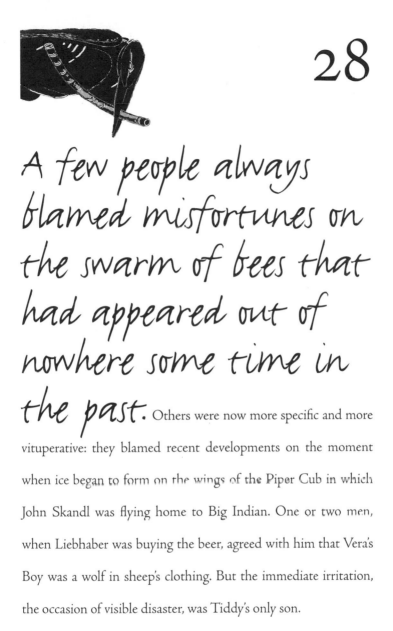

28

A few people always blamed misfortunes on the swarm of bees that had appeared out of nowhere some time in the past. Others were now more specific and more vituperative: they blamed recent developments on the moment when ice began to form on the wings of the Piper Cub in which John Skandl was flying home to Big Indian. One or two men, when Liebhaber was buying the beer, agreed with him that Vera's Boy was a wolf in sheep's clothing. But the immediate irritation, the occasion of visible disaster, was Tiddy's only son.

John Gustav, because he could only walk in a figure eight, was never allowed out of the house. His body had grown to the size of adolescence and yet he had never uttered a sound. His face was as innocent, as untouched by time, and as flawlessly handsome as it was the day Tiddy took him home from the hospital.

One morning when Theresa O'Holleran went to air the parlor, the wind ripped the doorknob from her hand; it tore the door right off its hinges. Theresa went skipping away to find someone who might help her nail it in place. JG stepped into the empty doorway.

He had never felt the wind before. It lifted his arms, made them flap and flail. He laughed. JG burst into silent laughter, his innocent face bright with simple joy. It was a fall day, the air both cool and warm; the air itself told him to move.

JG stepped down off the doorjamb, into the drying pigweeds and the few sweet pea vines that had reached beyond their binder twine supports. Even before his right foot found the rotting step, he was moving. He veered right, leaving the doorway; he walked around the corner of the house, found his way under the clothes-line wires into the garden. He tramped his way through the carrots, through the beets, through a corner of the bean patch; he knocked over a head of cabbage; he continued all the while, to complete the first half, the swung portion and its reversal, of his figure eight. It would have been the most magnificent figure eight of his life, the best ever; it might, it must, include in one circle the house, in the second the garden. He pushed through a stand of corn, the stalks bending, breaking, to his relentless progress. The garden reached toward the bank that overlooked the river valley. At the bottom of the garden was the brown-twig poplar, grown huge now, its long, stiff-pointed branches moving in the wind.

JG had never seen a tree. He realized, in the instant of his confrontation, it did not block his going at all; it was a pathway into the sky. JG was not guilty of thought. It was a simple knowing that took him where he went. He had seen his only friend, the black crow, leap from an open window, into that same blue air.

Through the yellow-green dazzle of leaves, JG hoisted his white, heavy body. His arms had hardly learned their own muscles. His bare feet curled innocently against the green bark of the tree's trunk, against the pitted branches. His fingers found the hard consolation of knot and limb.

Theresa O'Holleran returned to the parlor door with her great-grandmother, Old Lady Lang. They carried between them a claw hammer and a handful of nails. They were already wrestling the door back into position, preparing to nail it permanently into place, when Theresa noticed the black crow, perched and napping on the back of a chair. Theresa stepped into the parlor; she was talkative herself and liked to philosophize with the crow, liked to tease it about becoming too fat, too lazy. She saw a jigsaw puzzle, incomplete, in the middle of the floor: it was a picture of a tree, in autumn colors, the air about it full of birds.

JG was climbing, higher and higher, up the trunk of the huge old poplar at the foot of the garden. He balanced on a thinner branch, reached higher.

JG tried to step directly into the sky, in imitation of his only friend, the black crow. Theresa and Old Lady Lang saw that much. They saw him flap his arms and step out into the blue air, and they shouted, both of them, high-pitched and almost screaming; helplessly they shouted. Theresa dashed through the garden, leaping over the pumpkins that lay almost concealed under broad green leaves; Old Lady Lang, one hand in a pocket of her apron, followed after, at once trying to call out and to catch her breath.

JG himself made no sound; he made not a sound, not even as he plummeted, except that his heavy body ripped and tore its way through the outer branches of the tree and thudded onto the ground. He fell into one of Rose O'Holleran's graveyards. Whether it was the fall itself or the half dozen pointed crosses on which he was impaled that killed JG, no one ever quite decided for certain. He was simply dead.

The black crow, according to all reports, flew away, flew south, that very day. It had recently taken to napping a lot, especially after meals. Some people claimed that as it left it called out, one last time, "Total asshole." Most people argued that it left without saying a word; it flapped up into the sky; it flew, tossed and torn and ragged, the way any crow flies, into the wild shuffling of the everlasting wind.

29

The funeral was held
in a blinding dust

storm. Father Basil insisted that JG be given a child's

funeral. The body was preceded out of the church toward the

graveyard by a boy carrying a white, wooden cross. But the pall-

bearers, young boys let out of school for the morning, were not

strong enough to carry the fat white coffin all the way. Six grown

men had to step in and help; the wind blew and threatened to lift

them all now, lift them up and sweep them away. Tiddy followed

along behind the dusty white coffin, supported, as before, as

always, by Liebhaber's helping arm. She held on, with one hand,

to the skirt of her black coat. The dust and tears mingled in the

corners of her eyes. Sometimes she cried. Sometimes she thought

of the smell of shit in her parlor and how, finally, she'd be able to

scrub the room clean.

The wind blew the flowers off the casket. It blew dust into
Father Basil's face when he tried to intone a prayer. It blew the
clay off the shovel when Leo Weller threw down the first shov-

elful onto the lid of the wooden roughbox; it was Leo, glancing into the grave, who noticed the first salamander. He buried it out of sight with the second shovelful of clay.

The mourners, going out to Tiddy's farm for a drink and a bite to eat, noticed more of the same small reptiles. Hardly six inches long, looking as dry as dust, their splotched bodies might have passed for sticks on the road, had they not, slowly, moved.

All that day salamanders came by the thousands. It wasn't their breeding season. It wasn't anything that anyone could explain; the mourners at Tiddy's house shook their heads and filled their glasses. Someone blamed the wind. Someone said it was the departure of the black crow that did it. One man, drunk, went so far as to hint that Old Lady Lang had something to do with the invasion; she looked vaguely like a lizard. People called them lizards. Only Vera, working on her column of district news, ignoring the crowd in the house, gave them their right name. Vera believed that everything should be given its right name: salamanders, she insisted.

They crawled through the dust and dead grass of the yard, moving with a solemn, preposterous slowness. And yet there were so many, no human effort could turn them back. The wheels of departing cars crushed their way through writhing salamanders, churned the yard into strings of torn guts, into a mishmash of bulging eyes and random legs and tails. But still they came, olive and gray and green, in the failing light. They swarmed invincibly around the house, into the garden. They found their way into the cellar; the dark of the cellar filled with crawling salamanders. The water tank, out by the windmill, in front of the barn, was full of swimming salamanders. Tiddy, that night, found one in her bed.

During the night the plague ended. By next morning the stink of death was beginning to ripen on the endless wind. Vera Lang had composed an eloquent defense of the helpless little creatures for her column of district news; she praised their soft, moist, scaleless skin; she liked their slow gentleness. But the men who were assigned to empty the tank of bloated corpses, to scrape them out of the yard, to gather them into buckets with their bare hands in the cellar, those men, after an hour, insisted it was women's work. They left the cleaning up to the women. They remembered that the hunting season had begun.

A dozen district men went out to shoot ducks around Isador Heck's big hay slough. They sat all afternoon in their blinds, waiting, hardly daring to move a muscle for fear the slightest motion would scare away the ducks. Not daring even to talk, they began to imagine that salamanders came up out of the water, up their pantlegs. They watched the horizon. They tried not to flinch. They were sure they felt salamanders crawling into the baggy crotches of their water-proof pants, up onto their hunched backs.

All afternoon the wind blew with such ferocity that the ducks couldn't get down out of the sky. They came over the horizon, flock after flock. The men were reluctant to go home, not wanting to confront the stink of death. The flocks of ducks came over the horizon, grew larger, passed overhead, grew smaller.

How the first battle in the war against the sky began was never quite made clear. It was almost sundown when someone fired a shot at the wind. It was argued later that the buckshot flew back in the hunter's face and surprised him into firing again. The ducks were nowhere within range of the shotguns, everyone agreed to that. The cold wind was numbing; the endless sound of the mallards overhead was irritating to the waiting men; perhaps it wore on their nerves and made them trigger-happy. Whatever the case, the men in the next blind, hearing the first two shots, opened fire; then some hunters farther along the edge of the slough, hidden in stooks of wheat, waiting for the ducks to come down to feed, hearing the gunfire out of nowhere, opened up with a blast of their own. The wheeling ducks, frantic to land against the wind, so filled the air they darkened the setting sun. Smoke, suddenly, poured from the blinds and stooks and the trenches and was snatched away by the wind, was blended with the smoke that drifted across the slough from the west: somewhere a farmer had been reckless enough to try and burn stubble. The firing punctuated the endless nagging of the wind. A mudhen, trying to land, was shot to pieces; three dogs broke loose.

That night in the beer parlors along the flyway, word of the Battle of Heck's Slough spread like wildfire. The men around the beer tables should have been muddy, wet, smeared here and there with blood. Instead they had a dusty look: their hair, their faces, their shirts, their pants and boots all wore the look of dust. Instead of talking of mallards and pintails, the spent men told of a roof lifted off a barn; of a granary lifted out of a field and rolled across a road. They told of the sight of whirlwinds, dancing out onto the water, of prairie fires getting out of hand. The wind was gaining ground against them; they drank their beer, thirstily, wiped dusty hands across their mouths, and they knew the wind was gaining ground. One man had sprained an ankle while trying to run for cover. Another had nearly drowned when his shotgun knocked him out of the tiny boat in which he was concealed under a covering of cattails.

It was that same night that the black crow was first quoted as an authority. Men asked each other, what did the crow say about the flight of birds in a high wind? What did it say about salamanders? They wished the crow hadn't left them; they wanted to ask all the questions they'd neglected to ask while the crow was in their midst. And even while the crow had been talking, meditative and wise, they'd neglected to listen, they realized. Now and then someone claimed to quote the black crow on the subject of women or of guns.

Next morning, in the far southern reaches of the municipality, where the open stretches of prairie around the sloughs and lakes made for good goose hunting, a skirmish broke out at dawn. Hunters who had lain concealed in the dark, drinking whiskey and waiting for the geese, heard the first call, the first high honking, over the endless sawing of the wind.

The sky, from the northern horizon to its zenith, was filled with vees of geese. One man counted fifty-nine vees of geese in the clamoring air; the geese came like a great dead tree, dragged across the sky. The sound was unbearable to the frustrated men; not one goose could come down, against the wind. Sleepless, crazed with frustration, the waiting hunters opened fire.

The Battle of Twelve-Mile Coulee, it came to be called. One man was carried into the Big Indian General Hospital with his kneecap shot away. Two men developed piles from lying through the night in a ditch full of muddy water. At least four cases of pleurisy and pneumonia were traced, later, to that one battle. The women of the Municipality of Bigknife, from the Indian reserve in the north to the Hutterite colony in the south, began to prepare for a long siege; they began to roll bandages; they took home from the general stores and from the pharmacies extra rolls of tape, extra cotton batting, extra iodine and Mercurochrome.

Father Basil, the following Sunday, preached a sermon against the empty sky. He was not a hunter and hadn't noticed the endless flights of ducks and geese, he saw only the cloudless sky. "We've got to bust her loose," he shouted, raising his old fists over the altar railing. Men and women wept in their pews at the old priest's eloquence. Hardly a farmer had got his seed back out of the stunted stalks of grain. Cows in the dry fields looked gaunt and sick. Children, dazed, bewildered by the endless wind, came home from school and crept into bed. Father Basil spoke of the vast and windy constipation of the universe itself. The sky, empty; Father Basil, raging now. He developed the metaphor of the constipated universe; he entered into a kind of heresy, a vast doubting of God's perfection. He nodded his head of bushy hair at his own wisdom. "John Skandl wasn't as dumb as he looked," Father Basil added, humbly. "If the soil keeps drifting, we'll need his lighthouse this coming winter."

Liebhaber, at the mention of the lighthouse, remembered his own last memory of the future; he was absent-minded and had nearly forgotten it. He was sitting upstairs where he could look out of a window. He left the pew in such a hurry he almost pitched forward over the low balcony at the top of the narrow stairs. He poked at the holy water font and missed it completely. He hurried out into the empty sunshine. He walked and jogged and ran toward the river. He was at the river's edge again.

It was obvious to Liebhaber: a terrible flood was on the way. A flood was coming as surely as the salamanders had sought higher ground. Fish would swim in the streets of Big Indian. Liebhaber almost liked that idea.

He found the perfect place, near John Skandl's deserted granary. He picked up a willow stick and marked in the dust, at the river's edge, in the actual bed of the river, the water was so low, he marked the shape and size of the keel. It was time to start building a boat; he marked the place and the outline. Then he went to find Joe Lightning; they had talked once, the two men, years ago, though Liebhaber couldn't remember what the topic had been.

Joe Lightning was the only other man in the district who wasn't at war with the sky. He was the descendant of warriors; he knew when not to fight.

30

Day after day, night after night, the wind blew. It was a prairie wind, from the southwest, a ferociously hot, dry wind that came like sandpaper at the eyes of the men trying to harvest wheat. It exhausted the women, out in their gardens, trying to break cobs of corn from the rattling stalks, trying to dig enough potatoes for supper, to gather their cukes before a damaging frost. The dust worked into the pores of everyone's skin: human skin turned gritty and gray. The blown dirt found its way through closed windows, filled curtains with gray dust, covered furniture with fine, gray dust. Getting into bed at night, the exhausted citizens found dust on their pillows.

They were growing older. All the people in the Municipality of Bigknife could feel themselves, each day, growing older. It was unbearable after a few weeks. The sound of the wind, all night, was filled with age. The fields lifted up; slowly, the fields lifted, faded off into the sky. Tiddy, one afternoon, switched on the yard light at two o'clock. Her granddaughter, Theresa, looking at herself in the mirror in the parlor — they could use the parlor now; it no longer smelled of shit, it smelled of dust — Theresa said, "Look," — she put her hands over her beautiful cheeks — "I'm growing old."

Everyone was growing older by the hour. It was that calamity that drove Joe Lightning into his resolve to act. He was a man afflicted with memory. He alone, in the whole municipality, remembered JG; or at least he alone honored the memory. He remembered riding his horse to the parlor window for a rendezvous with Cathy, and confronting instead JG with his everlasting look of innocence. Tiddy told one person in the whole world that JG sang in her womb. Before he was born he had the habit of singing. Tiddy told that secret to Joe. Only at the moment of birth did JG fall into his terrible silence.

Joe thought of the boy often, throughout the winter. Sometimes, working with Liebhaber on the boat, he was tempted to ask questions about the boy's paternity, about his mysterious need to sing. Sometimes, at night, curled up in his car body beside Cathy — they had moved back into town — he asked himself the question: what if the boy had actually succeeded? What if, stepping from the top of the tree, he had entered the sky?

Joe Lightning was opposed to the war against the sky; he believed in the union of the elements. By early spring he had made his plan. He went into a coulee a mile upstream from town, not far from the Lang farm. He dug a pit and covered it with pussy willows. Then, on top of the willows, he tied a live bush rabbit by one leg.

Joe crawled into the pit beneath the rabbit and the pussy willows. He knelt, for three days, looking up, waiting. Sometimes at night he went home for a few hours, to Cathy. He told her he was helping Liebhaber build his boat; Joe was the only person in the world willing to help Liebhaber; he liked the elements, earth, air, fire and water. He had a plan for learning the sky's own secret.

On the morning of the fourth day it happened.

The eagle, seeing the weakened, struggling rabbit, swooped down. Joe Lightning was on his knees, poised, ready. He reached through the covering of pussy willows. He seized the eagle by the legs. Or by the talons, if not the legs.

It was Joe's intention to wrestle the eagle to earth and drag him into the pit. Somehow he would communicate with the eagle, as

JG had communicated with the black crow. He would learn about the sky. That was his intention.

The eagle was stronger than Joe. Joe was strong. But he was also small. He had a slight beer belly but he was, nevertheless, small. He struggled heroically, then suddenly found himself lifted out of the concealed pit.

Joe hung on for a minute too long. Before he knew it, he was looking down on the town of Big Indian.

What he saw, from his strange perch, high in the air, was never discovered. He had spent his life in the horizontal world of shuffleboards and pool tables and prairie. Perhaps he could no longer tell them apart. He had many sayings for dealing with what went right or wrong on a shuffleboard. "Malfunction at the junction" meant he'd gauged an angle wrong. "Too late for a date" meant he should have pushed just a little harder before he let go the rock. "Wrong direction for an erection" meant he'd made a wrong guess from the start. Joe Lightning spoke the language of the beer parlor; he tried a few expressions on the eagle. "Malfunction at the junction," he said. He looked down.

What looked like a fish, far below him, proved on second glance to be the back of a cow. Joe was having that kind of trouble with his expectations. He concentrated. He recognized the railway track, gleaming its way into the valley, across the river on what had to be a bridge, up again, onto the reaching plain. The grid of roads shaped the fields. He was surprised at how small the town looked, the once immense town where he'd been ignored, insulted; perhaps that recognition occasioned his first laugh. He was able, even, to single out the car body that was his; Cathy had painted it purple and gold. He watched for Cathy. He wanted to surprise her. He wanted to wave and only then did he realize he could not quite tell if he was holding the eagle, or the eagle's talons were holding him. It was that kind of question.

He was surprised at how awkwardly the eagle flew. From the ground, marveling for three days, he'd come to believe the eagle moved in a sky that was feather smooth. Now the great bird flapped and struggled. Both he and the eagle were jarred and lifted by currents of air, buffeted, dropped of a sudden. In that first, high circling, he began to sense the effect of summerfallow, of pasture, of a coulee's lip on the fickle air. He began to feel a little uncertainty about the eagle's skill.

Joe Lightning had time to reflect. He missed the consolation of a shuffleboard rock, small and round and hard in the palm of his hand. The talons were tearing his skin; he was as proud and vain, in the matter of his hands, as Liebhaber; they had talked a lot, the two men, trying to build a boat the like of which neither had ever seen. Joe's hands could measure speed and weight, control direction, create the absolute of concentration before release. But his hands were hardly his own now. He feared looking up more than he feared looking down. The town was turning. The air was so thin and blue it hardly filled his lungs. He needed to fill his lungs, he knew that.

His fall was as new to him as his rise; the vertical world was all a mystery. Nor was he certain whether he let go of the eagle or the eagle let go of him. He was adrift, he knew that much. The world was no longer floating away. The town was growing larger.

The laughter of his falling was heard over most of the district. It was more a laugh than anything like a cry of terror. And yet it maddened a horse in a nearby field: the horse ran head-on into an abandoned threshing machine and broke its neck. The gophers that sunned themselves, that Sunday morning, dived squeaking into their holes and did not return to the earth's surface, some people claimed, for a total of three days.

It was a simple laugh of pleasure and yet it was a kind of scream too, a scream of release. Joe, in his mile-high fall, with his arms spread like wings, his torn hands bleeding — perhaps, after all, he did learn something of the eagle's secret. Joe Lightning, whose only and purest knowledge was of a shuffleboard. He, the Shuffleboard Champion of the Great Plains, heralded and acclaimed in the air-conditioned beer joints of Nebraska; in the ranching towns of Montana, where cowboys emulated his wild, easy style; in the Lethbridge Hotel, where drunk Blood warriors challenged Hutterite patriarchs to a game for a round of beer; in the Indian beer parlors in Regina, where the magic name of Joe Lightning made brawlers put down their broken beer bottles; in the small towns of Alberta — Pincher Creek, Lacombe, Hanna, Smoky Lake, Oyen, Whitecourt, High Prairie, Milk River, Stoney Plain — where ranchers and farmers and oilfield workers watched the sky for rain and drank draft and dreamed of one day challenging the champ himself; at the thousand crossroads in Saskatchewan, where men stopped their pickup trucks and chatted of the games won the night before, of the games to be won the coming night, and then peed in a dry ditch, and then bragged again; in Flin Flon, where miners came up out of the rock itself; in Gimli, where fishermen came with burned, sore eyes off the endless reach of the lake; in the crowded pubs of Calgary and Edmonton and Saskatoon and Winnipeg where tall, blonde women, dressed for the heat, bent full-breasted and brassiereless over the shuffleboard tables, concentrated, reached, let go, imagining all the while their hero: Joe Lightning.

Some people, years later, believed they heard from the sky a version of prayer, a kind of holy laugh. Others, when insanely drunk, or on their deathbeds, admitted to hearing a laugh of such absolute obscenity they'd refused, for a whole lifetime, to acknowledge it. Some people, that same day, the day of the fall, began to argue that he'd flown up there on his own, Joe Lightning, cocky little Cree that he was; he was entirely responsible for his own fate. Others claimed to have seen a bird like none that ever existed on earth, a huge, flailing, long-legged bird the color of dust. They predicted a rash of victims.

Joe Lightning landed on the ladies' outhouse behind the Church of the Final Virgin. Or, rather, he landed where the outhouse should have been. Pranksters, the previous Halloween, had set it behind the toilet pit.

Joe Lightning, actually, might have been saved. He was still alive, still moving, eyewitnesses admitted, after his landing; the people who rushed out of the church, when they heard the laughter from overhead, actually saw Joe Lightning splatter a ton of shit and piss and catalogue paper over thirty-four parked cars. Joe Lightning might still have been alive, after his abrupt return to the earth. There was, a doctor from the General Hospital determined later, not a bone in his body broken. But the churchgoers, at the time of the fall, had on their Sunday clothes.

31

Liebhaber, hearing the laugh, the cry, looked up from where he was hammering nails inside the completed hull of his boat. He no longer went to church on Sunday; he had no time. He stood up, expecting to step onto the small dock that floated beside his hull. Intending to study the mystery of the laughing sky, he put his right foot on the gunwale. The wind was gusting. The choppy waves added their impetus to the gusting wind and to Liebhaber's natural gesture.

The hull turned over. Liebhaber was on the river alone, working alone. He fell inside the turning hull. He had no time to glance away from the bright sky before he was trapped into darkness. He was trapped in the air bubble under the completed hull of his half-completed boat; Liebhaber, his outcry muffled by water and wood.

He couldn't swim a stroke. He clung to a rib of the hull, kicking wildly with both legs, almost dog paddling. He heard the echo of his shouting, inside the watertight hull; his panic roared in his ears. He felt his right fist smashing against the neat boards.

Somewhere, in the midst of his terror, his frenzy, he realized he was staying afloat. By kicking vigorously, by clutching at the invisible ribs of the hull, of the darkness itself, he was managing to keep his head above water. But he noticed too that his breath came in hard, lumpy gasps that hurt his throat; obviously he was suffocating, there in the small bubble of air beneath the hull. He was running out of oxygen. He'd been there a long time, so long he hardly remembered ever being anywhere else. He struck again at the tight darkness over his head; he broke his nails, clawing; for all the cold of the water, he could feel the tearing of his nails on the lid over his head.

He remembered the laughter that came from the sky and he cried out in response, he screamed, he hollered, he groaned. He was becoming hoarse, he could tell that, and he feared his own exhaustion. Still kicking, his legs weaker now, his breath coming in harder gasps, he tried to listen. He expected to hear the insane, far laugh.

He heard the bird on the upturned hull. He heard the hard click of the bird's claws, on the hull, the knock of its beak at the rounded hull.

And then he thought of the bloodsuckers. Surely it was too early in spring for bloodsuckers. But he felt something on his thigh, something darker than the dark around him, shapeless, swelling itself to the shape of his blood. He felt something inside his shirt. He tried to claw at his own skin, under his clothing. The bird stopped moving.

The crow. He would know that sound anywhere, the certain, final sound of the black crow's walk. Liebhaber, knowing absolutely that the heavy-footed bird on the upturned hull was JG's black crow. The springtime return. The black crow, feeding on anything. Come to peck at his unseeing eyes. Liebhaber, in his wild fear, daring against the obscene hunger: "We are friends, black crow."

He pleaded now. To the black crow, perched on the hull, in the hot morning sunshine, eating waterbugs and bloodsuckers and worms: "Please," he whispered. "Old friend. Old comrade of the hard days." Then he knew his whisper would not be heard, and he raised his voice, still pleading, still deferring: "Please, black crow. Go to the church. Tell Tiddy."

The bird made no sound. Perhaps it had gone to deliver the message; Liebhaber, alone again, only his own words drumming in his ears. He listened. To the appalling silence. To the sea roar of his own blood in his own ears.

The bird moved again, on the hull. The claws clacked on the hull. The black crow hadn't gone to deliver the message. Liebhaber began to babble and cry, to whimper and scream; Liebhaber, almost insane at the everlastingness of his being trapped, hollering, demanding: "Black crow. Bugger off. Go get them, you total asshole. Get everybody. Bring them here. Go get everybody."

He listened, kicking, threshing, exhausted now, his grip on the wet rib slipping, holding again; he tried to listen. He'd been there forever.

But he had escaped too.

Liebhaber, trapped in the absolute darkness under the boat, trapped into death, hit on the realization that he had escaped. He hung onto a rib, in the cold water, trying to remember a life he hadn't lived. Without Gutenberg's curse; yes, that was it; without Gutenberg and movable type, he would have lived another life. And finally he was free of Gutenberg. I *perish*, he imagined, *but only in a dream*. No, that wouldn't do for an opening. Yes, he was writing his own story, at last. He tried again, working with furious intent: *Enough would be enough*. He liked that. He could account for events, announce the presence of design, under the apparent chaos. *Enough*. That one, sufficient word, so neatly balanced against itself. He had no idea how long he'd been under the hull. Perhaps it was night now. Surely someone would miss him. All night he would set type; everything set, everything forgotten. But now he had escaped; he had recovered the night, and dream, and memory. He would compose a novel one sentence long, a novel that anyone could memorize. *You in my arms*. Yes, that would do it. He tested for revision, recited the four words...

The crow's hard beak slammed at the hull. Liebhaber needed another sentence. "Please, dear crow, I take back everything." He couldn't stop; he was composing his novel. "I'll gather food for you. Grasshoppers and butterflies, wet with dew. I'll dig you cutworms, out of the soft earth. I'll pick you potato bugs. I'll steal young robins for you."

Silence. Silence, and only silence. A small lapping of water. He prayed for the plop of the crow's shit onto the wood above his upraised head. He'd been there forever. Under the boat. Trapped in darkness. He had no air to breathe. If his fingers, stiffened by the icy water, chanced to let him slip, he'd drown before he froze to death; he found that consoling. If it was night, then maybe it was dawn too. Maybe the crow had returned, benevolent and full of concern, out of the rising dawn. He was almost happy when the bloodsuckers inside his shirt found his armpits. His upraised arms exposed his armpits; he surrendered, letting them feast on his blood.

"Black crow?" he begged. "Is that you?"

No answer.

"Please, black crow. I can't last forever. I've been here forever. Is it morning?"

His voice was failing him. He realized his voice was gone blank. His pleading went silent from his lips. He heard the skittering of the bird's toes, on the top of his skull. He'd been there forever. He wanted to die. Liebhaber wanted to die; he let his right leg go limp.

Liebhaber's right foot touched the river bottom. The humiliation melted his arms. He shat himself. At that moment, against the constricting cold of the spring runoff, his sphincter opened; he felt the warm shit ooze softly into his underwear.

Liebhaber let go of the wooden rib, he dived a foot and a half into the muddy water, he surfaced

The morning sun blazed out of a spring sky. Liebhaber gasped for breath. He looked around to make sure no one was watching; the black crow was nowhere in sight. There were no birds anywhere. Yes, a few snipes dabbed along the shore, monstrously indifferent. A killdeer called, somewhere, invisible.

Liebhaber hauled himself up onto the dock. He tried to sit down and the shit spread through his trousers and he struggled to his feet. He found his watch in his coat on the dock; he'd been away nine minutes. He went home, shivering, not quite daring to walk straggle legged; he poured a triple shot of rye into his marmalade jar. He tried, for over an hour, to invent a new name for the black crow: traitorous coward, chiseling low-down thief, fountainhead of indifference, monstrous godhead of doom, three-legged child of a limping whore. He arranged the wooden type variously on his kitchen table, forever running out of the letters he needed most. He passed out in the can.

32

It was Joe Lightning's laugh of death that made Vera Lang decide to take a husband. She was stung by a bee at the exact instant of Joe's collision with the passing earth. For the first and only time in her life, she was stung. Out on a hillside west of town, beside a hive of bees, in the shelter of a poplar grove, she was squatted down. There were those, later, who argued that she was stung where it might most create a swelling and an itch. But she herself intimated that Joe Lightning, and he alone, in his lyric entertainment of the empty sky, made her relent.

They came from everywhere, the first candidates for that love. They came on horseback, on foot; they came in trucks, on motorcycles, in old VWs, in new Buicks. They spoke learnedly of the gentleness of Caucasian bees, of the intelligence of Italian bees. They had theories on the medical uses of bee venom, on how to control swarming, on where to winter a healthy stand. They dared to walk bare-handed, bare-headed, lifting a frame out of a brood chamber, examining a new queen.

And yet each of the first nineteen suitors, considering the bees that had once swarmed between Vera Lang's perfect thighs, was rendered totally impotent. Not one could transcend the limits of his own imagination. They came to her exquisite and inhuman beauty. They hesitated. They failed. They went away.

Marvin Straw, hopelessly in love, clinging to the crossbar of a telephone pole, peering out from a hole in a snow bank beside a road, skulking in a herd of cattle near a bee yard, waited in dumb attendance. But Vera ignored Marvin Straw.

She married, first, a handsome brute who worked for Alberta Government Telephones, burying cables. Marvin, in pathetic fear, in raw panic, watched the telephone poles come down. The crews stripped his perches of wire, lifted the poles flat onto the prairie grass along the country roads. The crawling yellow machine dug its trench and buried the bright new cable.

Ebbie Else, the man who operated the machine, a bulky, casual man who heard nothing that was said to him, liked to walk into the Big Indian beer parlor after a ten-hour day in the dust and heat and announce to one and all, "I'm so horny I could fuck a McCormick reaper." He laughed at the passion of Marvin Straw; it amused him so much that, one evening, acting from malicious- ness alone, he drove out toward the Lang farm to take down the pole that Marvin had climbed for his night's vigil.

Ebbie Else and Vera, fourteen hours later, eloped. They left in a van loaded with telephone equipment; they returned shortly with a stack of supers, two secondhand smokers, a big, modern extractor, dozen of empty jars, a new electric uncapping knife. Else was completely changed. He listened as if every rustle of a leaf, every drip of a tap, contained a message. He was nervous, uneasy, timid. He gave up drinking in the beer parlor; after working all day, burying cables, he'd rush to the farm. It was harvest time again, help was scarce.

And then the afternoon of total stillness made matters worse. Hardly had combining begun, in the bright fields of wheat, when the wind that had blown for months suddenly and briefly and absolutely died down.

There arose such swarms of horseflies, in the unexpected calm, that whole herds of milk cows, kicking up their heels, went through barbed wire fences. Horses galloped in wide, echoing circles around the dry pastures. Pigs, with no sloughs to wallow in, rooted frantically in the dust. Dogs leapt from the ground, seeming to snap at the air itself. A few citizens of the Municipal District, unable themselves to cope with the flies, fastened makeshift tails to the backs of their trousers or skirts and learned in a matter of minutes to switch them back and forth. Women, especially, took to wearing over their eyes forelocks in the manner of horses. One elderly gentleman figured out how to twitch his ears and the muscles of his thighs. And yet, for all the precautions, the afternoon constituted a veritable bloodletting.

Ebbie Else, when he finished work that day, drove directly out to the Lang farm. He went immediately, without stopping for so much as a cup of coffee at the kitchen table, to water the bull.

The slough near the barn had gone dry. The dugout in the middle of the Lang pasture had hardly enough water in it to float a pair of ducks. The shallow puddle was more green scum than water. Even the cattle outside the corral were ornery, cranky in their thirst. Else knew that; he pumped a pailful of water by hand — the windmill wasn't turning — and he carried the brimming pail through the barn, out to the corral.

But he could have set the pail through the gate. Why he entered a corral that enclosed a huge, restless bull and a swarm of stinging horseflies, that was not easy to decide.

Three boys, coming to play scrub with the girls on the farm, were witness from a distance to some of the tragedy; and yet their confused account of the lumbering man who ran in circles around the standing bull only added confusion to the argument that ensued. By nightfall, when the RCMP arrived and began to trace patterns of tracks in the dust around the torn corpse, by then it had become apparent, at least to some of the assembled farmers, that the bull was not entirely to blame. Vera, for the only time in her life, left an item out of her column of district news. But even so, for all her abrupt silence, the rumor began to spread: it was not the bull that charged.

Ebbie Else, in some unnameable agony, or fear, or desperation, had charged the bull. The corpse, at the wake, as if startled or afraid, three times sat up in the coffin. In the heat it began to smell, just faintly, and Vera asked that the vigil be held for one night only, that the funeral be set forward one day.

When she praised her dead husband — and she did so almost generously at times — she praised the bones of his body. She spoke, softly, erotically, of the full shape of his cranium, under the tangle of dusty hair. She admired the sharp, almost obscene beauty of his hipbones, the symmetry of his ribs, under the delicate skin. Then other suitors, the failed ones, attracted by news of the tragedy, remembered her gentle, firm hands and how she would caress the bones of a wrist, the line of a collarbone; how she would lift the knuckles of a thumb to her mouth and tongue. And none of them returned to the farm, not one.

33

Liebhaber, that same fall, finished building his boat.

And the day he completed it the river stopped running. He, walking in circles around the long, narrow hull with its high wheelhouse perched like an outdoor biffy, galumphing carelessly through the drying mud, raved for two hours and fifty-five minutes against the lunatic world. He stopped only when he glanced up at the yellowing trees along what had been the bank of the river and noticed Marvin Straw perched on a high branch, staring with hollow, maniacal eyes.

The wind had begun to blow again, after the brief reprieve. It blew all fall; it blew most of the winter. A closed-in cutter with a heater mounted on the front was turned over by the wind, on a bare stretch of road, and the boys who had witnessed Ebbie Else's death barely escaped with their lives from the spilled coals. The scared horse, pulling the flaming wreck, ran all the way into Big Indian where Liebhaber, watching from a window of the newspaper office, buried his head in his hands, refusing to see.

And yet the wind brought little snow; there was hardly enough to cover the fields. On a warm day, when the topsoil thawed, the summerfallow began to drift, clouding the winter gray and dull. It was the strange weather, Vera insisted, that killed most of her bees; she had always brought her colonies alive through the bitterest cold. It was the weather, too, a dust storm in the middle of winter, that killed her second husband.

The Adams boy from north of town had a face like a skull and most women didn't like him. He was a chicken thief by instinct, if not by trade. His father had courted Tiddy Lang; it was something of a family tradition, the courting of the Lang women. The younger Adams, almost out of a sense of obligation, proposed; and Vera, still in her widow's weeds, wearing a yellow scarf with her black dress, accepted.

When the young husband disappeared, almost all the men in the community entered, with a kind of fevered eagerness, into the search; but they searched the entire municipality without success. It was an Indian woman, pulling frozen fish out of a net with her bare hands, who chanced to notice the missing husband's shadow under the ice.

Sometimes the younger Adams, toward the end of winter, stole fish instead of chickens. What had happened to him was clear enough: he'd stepped into a hole in the ice while trying to rob a net in a lake on the Indian reserve. It seemed apparent that, because of a dust storm out on the lake, he hadn't seen the ice-crusted hole.

No one any longer remembered how to cut ice, except for one man who'd been the chickadee on John Skandl's cutting gang; he'd gone around behind the teams of horses picking up horse shit with a scoop shovel. He had some recollection of how to cut the blocks, how to bob one of them high enough for the grip of the big ice tongs, and he took on the job of retrieving the body. When he finished the cutting, when he lifted the blocks and was able to see beneath the cover of dust, he discovered that the body of the younger Adams was, due to the passage of time and the continued freezing, actually embedded in the ice which he had cut. He'd accidentally divided the corpse into four sections intersecting at the belly button, though he'd arranged the four principal blocks incorrectly on the surface of the frozen lake.

The curious thing was quite simply that the drowned man, allowing for errors in the reassembling, had apparently been swimming away from the hole through which he'd fallen. The four principal blocks were delivered to the Lang farm and again, purely by chance, arranged together incorrectly. Vera spoke strangely of the delicacy of chicken bones, of the symmetrical beauty of the bones of whitefish and pickerel.

Liebhaber went out to help the men who volunteered to dig the grave. The ground, because of the light snowfall, was frozen to a depth of four feet. The men who'd shown up by midmorning built a fire where the grave was to be. They squatted around the fire and warmed their hands.

The fire became a kind of beacon. It attracted the attention of other men who were passing by. One of them chanced to have a mickey of rye in the glove compartment of his car. Another had a case of beer in his trunk. Leo Weller, supervising, told someone to bring more firewood and a bucket of coal from the church basement; he paid for the next bottle out of his own pocket and sent two men to the government liquor store. The gravediggers drank while they waited for a few inches of clay to melt. Then they moved the fire a yard or two and dug in the thawed clay, their boots becoming huge pads, huge obscene weights. A cold wind was blowing; by late afternoon the grave was deep enough to be warm, sheltering. The men hunkered down inside, smearing their clothes, their gloves, even their faces now, with the clay.

They dug a hole that was more a crater than a grave. Leo Weller drove a pick into the grave's wall to make a niche in which to set a new bottle; it was he who first noticed the roughbox containing John Skandl's casket.

They were drunk, the men. Darkness had fallen. Liebhaber suggested they take a peek. At first the others only laughed. And then, before Liebhaber could explain, someone discovered that the fire had charred the roughbox, had burned through to a brass handle inside.

The night was pitch black, because of the drifting dust and snow. The lantern burned fitfully on the heap of clay above the grave. Liehaber actually tried to get out of the way by getting out of the grave, only to find he was too short, the clay too slippery. Bill Morgan and Alphonse Martz together were prying up the lid of the coffin when the face looked over the clay heaped at the edge of the grave.

When Marvin Straw spoke his greeting, when the men in the grave looked up and saw his maniacal eyes, his hunched, bony shoulders and his twisted face; when the love-haunted man accidentally put out the lantern by knocking it down into the grave, the inquest ended so abruptly that Eddie Brausen was left behind with three fingers of one hand caught under the coffin lid.

That night in the Big Indian beer parlor every man in the place spoke continually for two hours and fourteen minutes, not once pausing to hear what another had to say. Alphonse Martz asserted 108 times that gophers, digging down for water, had hit on Skandl's casket; then badgers, hungry for gophers…Bill Morgan, wiping at the empty socket of his missing eye, interrupted 108 times to report that part of the nose was missing, along with at least seven of the toes. Eddie Brausen, unwilling to admit that he'd been the slightest bit dismayed at being left alone in the grave, announced to every newcomer to the beer parlor that he sat and drank two bottles of beer that he found in the coffin. Leo Weller, trying to reassert his authority, observed to an empty chair that the lid of the coffin had been clawed, the satin ripped, by Skandl's own fingernails. Liebhaber, defiantly, before he passed out in the can, announced to anyone who came in to urinate that Leo Weller had to be a liar because the coffin was so full of hair there was no way to see Skandl's hands; Skandl's hair and beard had grown, filling every small space…

When the beer parlor closed that night the men went out shouting that they'd see each other in church.

And yet, next morning, not one person from the entire Municipal District of Bigknife voluntarily attended the funeral of the younger Adams. Mr. Aardt the undertaker was there of necessity, shivering, wrapped in a rug, pressing at his hernia. Father Basil had the assistance of one altar boy, who carried the holy water sprinkler in his left armpit. An ugly rumor began to circulate that same day, insinuating that Vera herself did not attend her husband's funeral. The mixture of dust and snow that blew in a cloud across the graveyard obscured all possibility of vision. Old Father Basil himself almost slipped into the crater when he chanced to glance down and saw dimly a scattering of picks and shovels, bottles, gloves, jackets, caps, wallets, eye glasses, buckets, claw hammers, crowbars, beer cases, and lantern parts, beneath the descending coffin.

34

It was the accident that befell Vera's third husband that gave Gus Liebhaber his finest idea.

The third husband — and Vera was careful that no one ever learned his name for certain — worked on a road gang. One of the provincial governments, or possibly both of them, had decided to build a highway through the Municipality of Bigknife. Because of the river valley, or perhaps because of a surveyor's error, it would pass two miles south of the town of Big Indian. But construction was actually in progress, the fields of a half dozen farmers had been ripped up and the clay had been piled into a long heap in the middle of the new road allowance, when the man in charge fell in love with Vera.

He was a tall, gangling man, the foreman, covered in dust from head to foot. Even after he'd attempted to wash, his ears were full of dust, his hairline was full of dust, the skin of his knuckles was dark with a mixture of grease and dust. His men knew he was in love because one day he had them build a grade through a slough; the next day he had them level it. The third day he put in a culvert on top of a hill. He tried, briefly, to reroute the road, over the river and past the Lang farm. He asked permission to transplant a country graveyard and sulked when he was refused. For ten days he went on like that, tearing up fields with bulldozers and carryalls, knocking down fences and trees. Then, one morning at coffee break, he saw a snake trying to copulate with a logging chain. The tall, gangling stranger with hair the color of dust took that as an omen. A sign. He was supposed to stop building roads and get married.

He and Vera went into town on a D-8; the stranger drove the big yellow Caterpillar down Main Street, to the Church of the Final Virgin. Father Basil heard them coming and was ready when they arrived. It was rumored they were married right there on the dusty seat of the D-8, the engine idling while Father Basil intoned. At any rate, the stranger backed the big Cat away from the church steps and took his new bride on a honeymoon. Pulling a bunkhouse and a cookhouse — the entire road gang had quit — they went on a tour of all twenty-four of Vera's bee yards, preparing them for a shipment of bees from California.

The wind, that spring, was worse than at any time during the winter. It was so strong that the windmill on the Lang farm went on turning even after it was shut off. By the time the newlyweds returned to the farm it was squeaking terribly. It squeaked, out there in the yard by the barn, up in the sky, like an animal caught in a trap, like a man being tortured. No one in the house could fall into a decent sleep. The children woke up crying. Rita spent one whole night writing a letter, rather than face her uneasy bed. Old Lady Lang played and lost six games of solitaire in the middle of the night. Tiddy, accidentally, not checking the clock, served breakfast at one in the morning.

The tall, gangling stranger with hair the color of dust got up from Vera's bed at three in the morning and went to see what might be done. He slipped downstairs from the attic room in his stocking feet. He went out into the squealing darkness.

The driver of the cream truck who first saw the figure on the wheel of the windmill, spinning and spinning, thought it was Marvin Straw. He thought Marvin had finally overreached himself, in his attempts to spy out Vera's approach and presence; the driver was tempted to let him suffer for a while, was tempted to teach him a lesson. Only out of the goodness of his heart did he go to awaken the sleepers in the house and he found all of them, though still in bed, awake and listening. The sound of the windmill had changed, they knew that.

People, before the day was over, would recall the afternoon, twenty-four years earlier, when the spring sunshine brought a swarm of bees to the district. They knew that bad luck came in threes. After the bees, the salamanders and the horseflies. After the death of Ebbie Else and the younger Adams...

It was not Marvin Straw on the turning wheel. Marvin appeared, briefly, out of the poplar bluff north of the barn. "Things are adding up," he whispered, hoarsely, to Old Lady Lang. She nodded. Marvin disappeared.

The man on the turning wheel was the tall, gangling stranger with hair the color of dust. There was no way to turn off the windmill, the wind was too strong. He spun, up there in the sparkling sky, his hair trailing behind his fixed head, one sock loose on a locked foot, his arms outspread.

It was Vera herself who, later, wrote up the story for the column of district news in the *Big Indian Signal*. She left her account unsigned, anonymous, and Liebhaber was decent enough not to let on to anyone; in fact, while setting the type, he deliberately left out a detail. He understood that the stranger, working on a road gang, expected to get up in the morning and grease machines; it was natural to him, that gesture. But Vera hinted in her version that the husband — the windmill lover, she called him — she claimed there was some suggestion, from his position on the turning wheel, that he'd leapt from the small stand by the gear box, had actually fastened himself onto the wheel, had let the wind paste him against the spinning blades.

"Is he still alive?" men asked each other, staring up at the spinning, squeaking wheel.

"Listen," someone said. It was Andy Wolbeck. He'd left his wife in charge of the railway station. Forty men, fifty, standing in the yard around the water tank, in front of the barn, tried to listen.

"Listen," someone said. "I think he said 'Help.'"

"Shhh," another man said, correcting the speaker. "Listen."

The women stayed in the house. The house was full of women; now and then a face appeared in a window, pale, drawn, curious; a face appeared, hesitated before it withdrew. The women in the house were taking care of the women in the house. They made coffee. They waited.

No one could figure out how to stop the turning wheel. Liebhaber looked about him and realized that every male over the age of sixteen in the Municipality of Bigknife had been injured or maimed or had suffered a related illness, in The War Against the Sky. Gunshot wounds had crippled grown men, robbed youths of fingers and toes. Exploding shotgun barrels had scarred handsome faces and ripped at biceps and elbows. Wise and confident men, driven to drink, had missed the curve in the road down into the valley, had sheared off powerline poles, had plunged over the banks of coulees, into boulders and gullies. One hundred and seventeen people had in six hours suffered horsefly bites. Hunters had turned over in boats, had been chewed up by the propellers of outboard motors; one group had clung all night, in rough water, to a drifting gasoline drum. Trees had fallen on the injured who sought shelter in the bush; the endless wind had lifted granaries and haystacks before astonished eyes, had grimly worn the sanest citizens looney.

"Help," the spun man called, or seemed to call, against the outrageous creaking of the windmill. The men on the ground were certain they'd heard him call out. His long hair, dust-colored, streamed in the wind behind his burnt, fixed head. His feet, now, were bare, burnt red by the sun and the wind.

Liebhaber, looking away from the assembled and waiting men, looking up into the sun, seeing in the sun's eye itself the living man spun wildly, had his idea. If it was war the sky wanted, then he would give it war. The terrible, iron sound; the screeching machine that spun the man silent — Liebhaber, watching the stranger pinned to the sky, hit on a way to win immortality.

He, Gus Liebhaber, would be the war's victor. Unnoticed, he ducked into the car shed where Vera kept her ancient Essex and her beekeeping supplies. He groped, at first, in the sudden dusk; he found an old sickle, a grape basket full of bolts and nails, an anvil on a great block of wood, a wine jug full of oil, a spare blade for the windmill. It was April; somewhere in the car shed were the packages of bees, newly arrived, that would restock Vera's 576 empty hives, at twenty-four different locations throughout the Municipal District of Bigknife. All her 576 new queens were there, each queen in a tiny cage, the cage suspended by a wire inside the wood and screen package. In each package were something like seven thousand bees; millions and more millions of waiting bees were stored in the cool and the dark of the car shed: Vera Lang's entire fortune and her life's work too, her dedication, her passion.

Liebhaber loaded the Essex full of packaged bees. He lifted open the car shed doors, the big, wooden doors themselves long ago slammed loose from their hinges by the wind. He climbed into the jam-packed car and managed to start the engine, managed to find reverse. He drove, as carefully as he was able, through the crowd of silent and listening men. Not one of them heard the car. Not one of the men in the yard, head tilted back, sweating, staring, looked away from the man imprisoned on the sky.

35

Isador Heck proposed to include himself into heaven. To that end he'd built a cannon of the sort he'd been shot from while traveling with the circus. He'd had a terrible argument with Father Basil who believed there is an after-life but who refused to acknowledge there is a place where it might be lived. Heck countered with his conviction that anything that can be imagined exists.

Heck had built the cannon, had even fired a few trial shots. But he couldn't decide when to include himself. He had a lingering suspicion that time might be the one thing that didn't exist; time might be an agent of self-deception, the means whereby man explains to himself his own ignorance of the existence of every-thing else.

Heck was in Tiddy Lang's yard, staring up at the man on the windmill. He wondered what the man saw, from up there, his eyes white in his head. He was thinking of new arguments to present to Father Basil, who'd never been higher off the ground than the second storey of the Lang house.

Liebhaber drove out of the lane, turned onto the correction line road, and headed directly for Heck's tarpaper shack. He set in the first charge of bees just as the sun disappeared gaudy and red behind the horizon. The endless haze of dust in the air made the sky a lurid red, at sunset, the sun itself choking on dust. Liebhaber touched a match to the fuse, jumped out of the way.

The thunder of the explosion tore at his ears. The cloud of smoke, for a minute, more, obscured the ancient Essex from sight. The cannon was sheltered from the wind by the shack. Liebhaber, gasping and choking, groped his way through the smoke. He went to the barn for another washbasin full of powder. He fumbled into the cannon another charge of bees.

Liebhaber, that night, was set on gaining a victory over death itself, there in the manure in Heck's yard. The powder was stored in a back stall. Liebhaber flailed his way through the flies, through the stink of burnt powder and manure and rotting flesh. Coming out through the low doorway he banged his head on an upright pole, shook the dead hawk that hung from the pole by a length of barbed wire, the dead bird rising to claw his face. He freed with a pair of pliers the queens from their cages; he loaded the freed queens, with their thousands of smoke-stilled bees, into the cannon's throat.

Liebhaber, in the sweat of his need, stooping and rising, stooping and rising, would fertilize the barren sky. Gus Liebhaber, his quick hands finding more powder, finding more bees, striking a match, lighting a fuse. Liebhaber, in love, holding his hands to his aching ears, his eyes watering themselves blind; in the long, blind fury of his love, stooping and rising; in the passion of his greatest scheme, in his night-long and greatest fury against the death of the world, Liebhaber, shelling the crimson and careless sky; shelling the red sky black; alone and alone, he charged his gun. He lit the fuse. He waited out the heavy thud that knocked the night; and the myriad stars, they multiplied, as if his gun was setting them there. The far night, looming down. His bending and lifting back; his own small shadow of smoke, not quite so black now, lit by its own burst of flame; Liebhaber, aiming to crack the intricate knot of all his undoing. The fallen night, the high-flung bees, the rip of smoke, onto the silence. The clash of his own sounding, onto heaven's rim.

36

The first drops of rain fell on the hearse that was carrying Vera's third husband into Big Indian. The wind had fallen off toward morning; the waiting men had lowered the corpse with long ropes. The tall, gangling stranger from the road gang was hardly more than a bag of bones, he'd been so dehydrated, so perfectly dried. He was for a moment a kind of dried flower in Vera's arms.

Mr. Aardt, surprised by the rain, swerved, hit the ditch, swung back onto the road. He missed Marvin Straw by inches; Marvin was waiting in a stand of last year's cattails, his dirt-rimmed eyes feverish with love, feverish with renewed hope at the sight of the loaded hearse.

As the clouds thickened, moving eastward, they robbed the powerline poles of their shadows. Liebhaber, by this time, was lying on the deck of his boat; the boat was resting on dry land, where the river once had run. He'd been looking up at the sky for three hours and twenty-one minutes when he felt the first drop of rain.

He'd spent himself in the night of his secret warring. His back and his legs and his arms ached. Only slowly did he stir. The air was almost still, the wind had almost ceased from its endless blowing. And more: there came, now, the weighing of dark cloud onto the radiance of sky.

A drop of rain hit him and he knew it would be a flood. At last, his marriage time had come. He had remembered the future correctly: there would be a flood, a joy of rain, his battle won, his ark floating. Let the doubting bastards drown, he would save whom he pleased. He shook his head, wiped a drop of rain from his forehead, got to his feet.

Liebhaber drove Vera's Essex back to the farm. The few drops had become a drizzle by the time he got there. "It's going to rain cats and dogs," he shouted, hardly up the steps and onto the porch. It was not Tiddy, but Vera who first came to the door. She didn't bother to look at her Essex, returned, finally, from wherever Liebhaber had taken it. She said nothing of his theft, his vast conspiring to unhinge the world; he might have been, for all her attention, innocent.

And then, only then, did Liebhaber notice: here and there, with the falling drops of rain, fell a bee. Here and there a bee fell. Tiddy came to the door, now, and with her, Rose. Rose, as homely as she had always been, her shoes not tied, her dress not quite fitting. And with her the younger daughter, whose shoes were not tied, whose dress did not quite fit. But the older daughter was there too, Theresa O'Holleran, so beautiful, in the swelling of her young breasts, in the defiance of her blue eyes, that Liebhaber tugged at a corner of his mustache, for a moment caught it into his mouth.

Anna Marie came out onto the porch, with the others. She too saw the rain, knew that her hair, in a matter of hours, would be frizzy, unmanageable. Her youngest daughter came onto the porch and took the comb from her mother, began to comb her own dark hair, watching all the time the weather. Gladys Wurtz was there too, dressed in her Hutterite garb, no makeup on her pale face, the long skirt not quite hiding her heavy black shoes. She held her daughter's hand and the daughter held in her free hand a red ball. And Cathy came out too, Cathy Lightning stepped out onto the porch; she was making macaroons; she carried a bowl and an eggbeater. Only Rita was missing when the women praised the rain, when they invited Liebhaber into the house, insisted that he enter.

Vera stayed on the porch. "I'll go water the bull," she said. Sometimes, at any time of day or night, she went out to the windmill and filled a pail with water and carried it through the barn, out to the corral behind the barn, and watered the bull. But they knew already — not only Tiddy and Liebhaber, but the others too — they sensed it: the bees, coming down with the rain, were stirring Vera to a memory she could not quite control.

It was bees that stirred Vera. Vera Lang, finding the bees in the rain, the bees descending from the sky…

A bee landed on her bare shoulder. She was wearing a gold halter and a black skirt. She started to brush the bee away, then stopped. She caressed the fine hairiness of the bee.

Liebhaber followed Tiddy into the house. They sat down around the kitchen table, all the adults, the children pushing past them; everyone reached to the tray of overnight cookies that Cathy took from the oven. In the parlor, a TV set was turned too loud but no one was listening. All the talk was of rain. The talk was of green grass, of seeding, of crops. Of calves and cows in green pastures. Of getting the garden plowed, the potatoes planted. Of wheat rising into bright green rows on the rain-black land.

The rain drummed now on the roof of the porch. It drummed and sang against the chatter of the rhapsodic women. The wash of rain smeared the windows clean, came in a gust of wind to rap at the glazed windows, then came steady too, gave the steady promise of a long day's watering.

Liebhaber was silent while the women, in their new exhilaration, bantered, joked, filled coffee cups against the sudden cool of the spring air. He was scheming.

Liebhaber was about to propose. He was about to propose, for the thirty-third time, that Tiddy become his wife. He would remind Tiddy: she had said she would marry him when the sky opened, when the cloudburst came. He listened, his heart hammering in his chest, his lungs hardly daring to take in air, while the rain slammed the windows white with its hard falling.

He was about to speak — he was certain, after, that he'd been about to speak — when Theresa O'Holleran made her announcement:

"It's snowing," Theresa O'Holleran said.

The children, in their wonder, ran to the window to look.

The older women glanced from their coffee cups to each other's eyes. They remembered everything. Theresa was smiling an almost sly, uneasy smile. The older women remembered. Tiddy looked out over her granddaughter's head; she stared out of the window where once, so long ago, she had seen snow in June.

But it was Liebhaber who spoke. Liebhaber, his joy escaping him again; Liebhaber crying out:

"Who? *Who?* **WHO?**"

Theresa, matter-of-factly, added fresh cream to her coffee from the fat white pitcher. "It was a ghost," she said. She shrugged a little. "That's all."

Liebhaber slammed down a fist on the table and all the cups jumped. He roared an inarticulate roar, caught a corner of his mustache in his teeth. He knocked the hair out of his eyes.

"Someone must take a wife," Tiddy said. She was clearing the table, brushing at her apron. "Help with the dishes," she added, to no one in particular.

Theresa was the center of attention now and she wouldn't let her grandmother win so easily. She turned her head slightly, away from the table; Theresa O'Holleran was vain about her profile. "His legs went this way and that when he walked. I told him to lie down beside me." She gestured at the windows; the windows knocked blind by the sheets of rain. "It was there. Just past the big tree, at the foot of the garden. By the edge of the coulee. He came up out of the coulee. I was getting a suntan." Theresa sipped her coffee. "He was lonesome."

Liebhaber pushed his chair back from the table. He stood up and went to the door. He opened the door that led out onto the porch.

And then he did not step outside. He raised a finger, signaled the women around the table to be silent.

From the invisible sky came a sound. It was the sound of a machine. A machine, flying in the air, like a lost bee. The machine or its sound came at the house, passed over, came at the house, passed over again.

Vera Lang was gone from the porch, but Rita, now, was there, leaning out from under the protecting roof. She wasn't looking at the closed wooden gate. She ignored the two hens, wet, bedraggled, huddled under the caragana hedge. She was looking up at the sky.

They joined Rita on the porch, the other women. They could hear the machine, now, too. But they could see nothing. They began to chatter again. Only Rita remained silent as if she could, at last, in the wet air itself, sense a promise of doom and violation. "Listen," she said. She raised the eraser end of her ball-point pen to her lips. "Listen."

Liebhaber, muttering to himself, his hands in his pockets, went down the three steps; he went, bareheaded, into the pouring rain, away from the house.

37

Something was up there, after all.

The women in the Lang house went to bed that night with the rain falling, the machine in the sky periodically buzzing low over the house, going away, buzzing in close again, in the darkness and the rain. Theresa O'Holleran, saying her bedtime prayers, prayed to the sound in the sky that her child might be a daughter; men were a bunch of useless bastards. She said the same prayers, made the same request next morning, when she heard Vera's Boy, downstairs in the kitchen, talking on without listening, speaking a language she couldn't for the world understand.

Vera's Boy arrived just in time for breakfast; he was mud from head to foot. He leapt up and squatted on the edge of a chair, dripping mud and water onto the chair, onto the floor. Tiddy was furious, even before he spoke. He announced, with his mouth full of bacon, that the federal government had finally come to its senses and was using force to help in The War Against the Sky. Some tanks had joined the battle, he explained. He bit a slice of toast in half with one snap of his teeth.

"Don't speak with your mouth full," Tiddy said. She was trying to get the children fed and off to school, and the last thing she needed was a lecture.

Vera's Boy raised a fist at the ceiling. "I'll ipwhay every uckingfay loudcay up there," he buzzed and shouted. He had come to see the marshaled clouds as his enemies, closing ranks against him. "I'll ingwray them out. I'll urnbay their useless itstay ownday to the roundgay. I'll ryfay their asses."

"And watch your language in this house," Tiddy added.

Rose and Anna Marie were putting on raincoats and rubber boots, preparing to go out to feed the pigs and chickens and to do the milking. To humor Vera's Boy, to ease their mother's irritation, they said they'd go with him to see his forces at war in the valley. In fact they were worried because Vera wasn't in her bed, up in the attic.

Rose and Anna Marie followed Vera's Boy down through the vines and weeds of last year's garden, down to the valley's edge. To their surprise, an army camp had sprung up in the darkness of the night. A column of tanks clanked and crawled away from a row of neatly ordered olive-green tents. Vera's Boy squatted down on the edge of the clay-shouldered trench that was the valley of the Bigknife River. He gave a short, sharp yip, a kind of bark that almost became a howl. Squatted on his haunches, he held his head high, listening. He waved his arms, attempting to give directions, commands, to the moving tanks.

When the first shot was fired, Rose and Anna Marie had hardly time to recognize the artillery piece, under its camouflage, before the sky above them cracked open. A flight of F-104s swung down toward the valley, three planes in close formation, a fourth following; they screamed down recklessly close, then up into the air again, disappearing into the gray of the clouds. Vera's Boy howled. From far up the valley a coyote answered. The clouds were closing, coming down onto the earth as if wounded. The clouds bled rain.

The flight of F-104s, the screaming roar of the planes, brought Vera Lang up out of a coulee. She was soggy, wet, her wet clothing clinging to her body. She might have recognized her sisters, but then she spied a bee, on the dry side of a rock. She plucked the bee like a berry; she opened her large leather shoulder bag and dropped the bee inside. Now she forgot both the guns and the planes. She was collecting bees. They fell from the sky; they appeared, now and then, a bee on a saskatoon bush, on a strand of barbed wire, on the dry side of a willow fencepost. She gathered the fallen bees into her careful hands, into her bag. They were too wet to fly, the bees. Vera's desire was more than she could contain. Her eyes were bright, hot, intense when she met her sisters. She hardly knew them. She refused to go with them, back to the house. She touched her son. She actually touched her son's wet hair. Then she noticed another bee; she went to pursue it.

38

All day the rain fell.

The rain came in sheets at times, then it came as a long, slow drizzle, so fine in the air it seemed more a mist than a rain. Then the drops would grow again, swell, until the pelting rain on the house was a loud din.

Anna Marie went upstairs to look through her hope chest. She fingered her way through the collection of birds' eggs, of horse hair and dried mushrooms and thimbles and needles. She unwrapped the rabbit skin from her husband's testicles, the dried testicles cradled on a mallard's wing. Cathy was baking coffeecake; she liked to bake, on a rainy day. Gladys moved the rocking chair into the kitchen from the parlor, and sat and rocked, all the while crocheting a doily. The children stayed in the parlor, sitting on the floor where JG used to assemble his jigsaw puzzles.

Darkness came early, and in the valley the shooting stopped. Rita Lang sat at the dining room table by herself, trying to write a letter. She had never before had trouble writing a letter, but now she hesitated. She chewed at her ball-point pen and the ink marked her lips blue. She thought of her prisoners, in their narrow bunks, once more before lights out reading the letters that praised their pale bodies. Rita, caressing with words her faithful men.

All night the rain fell and in the morning the soldiers' camp, in the valley, was half under water. The big trucks and the trailers were mired in mud. The slow men, moving in the mud and the water, were the color of spring, green and brown, as if they too had, unwillingly, sprouted and grown in response to the insistent rain. Their tents looked like toadstools. The river was wide now, had lost its bed and its shape. The loud and spreading river moved into clumps of trees, oozed out over pastures and into dead oxbows. From under camouflage, a gun exploded the morning.

Early that same afternoon a hailstorm, unexpectedly, moved in a long, narrow streak along the valley. Lumps of ice, some of them the size of baseballs, hurtled from the sky. Often, inside a huge hailstone, was a bee, frozen into perfect stillness, magnified by the convexity of the encasing ice. The artillery unit fell silent. Three men sprawled motionless in the mud; they were carried by comrades in steel helmets to the first aid station.

39

It was the hailstorm that brought the young man to the farm. Darryl Dish was a seminarian from near Edmonton, employed for the season to chase hailstorms. He was to report on the velocity of the wind, the wind's direction, the size of the stones, the nature of the damage; he chased the storms wildly in a pickup truck. He jumped out of the truck, there in the Lang yard, dressed in his cowboy hat and running shoes, in his denim shirt and his tight, faded denim cut-offs. He picked up a dozen hailstones and raced to the door of the Lang house, leapt over the three steps and crossed the porch and almost went in at the door without knocking. Breathless he asked that the hailstones, immediately, be put in the freezer compartment of the refrigerator; Tiddy told Theresa O'Holleran to lend the young man a hand.

Darryl Dish, the heaped hailstones stinging his bare hands and arms, waited while Theresa shuffled ice cream cartons and popsicles and frozen vegetables and cans of orange juice. She fumbled, looking away from her chore; she noted again the running shoes that were tracking the floor, the hairy thighs, the tight cut-offs.

Rose O'Holleran came into the kitchen through the door that he had left open. She saw the flies, sluggish in the damp air, getting into the house, and was angry. She saw the hailstone chaser. He reminded Rose of her husband, who sometimes not only felt his missing leg and private parts, but could use them. He reminded Gladys of Eli the Hutterite, and how he plucked geese, and how he liked a feather tick on a rainy day. He reminded Old Lady Lang of the nameless Cree buffalo hunter after whom the first settlement had been named.

"What's that buzz?" Darryl said. He looked up at the ceiling as if he might see the sky.

They wanted the black crow to be there. All the women wanted to ask the black crow: what's that buzz, up there in the sky? The black crow would have told them.

Theresa O'Holleran, reaching to take a hailstone, accidentally touched Darryl's right hand.

"I'm Terry," Theresa said. She'd never in her whole life allowed anyone to call her anything but Theresa.

Rose O'Holleran crossed herself and started to make a novena.

Old Lady Lang was sitting on the wood box by the stove, keeping warm against the chill, letting down the hems on some skirts for two of her great-granddaughters. She licked the point of thread, bent close to find with the wet point of thread the eye of the needle. "It's too sad," she said. "Ach, *ja*." She thought of the buffalo hunter. "I don't want to think about it."

40

Jerry Lapanne, in his thirty-ninth attempt to escape from the penitentiary in Prince Albert, had invented a flying machine. In his passion and haste, however, he'd neglected to include in his invention a way to get back to earth. He'd been circling for two and a half days, in the clouds and mist over the Bigknife valley.

Word spread slowly through the rain-soaked town, up onto the farmland above the valley: a murderer, a sex-crazed Frenchman, was up there in the sky. The RCMP were looking, the army was looking, the air force was looking, and they'd been able to see nothing. But the people in the streets, the few men in the beer parlor, "He's up there," they said. They were on his side, finally, rooting for him against all reason. "He's up there," people said, as if he'd been there all along, but never seen. And just when the doubters began to win the arguments, someone would hear the machine again, the invisible machine in the sky.

Not a single person came to Liebhaber's boat. Everyone was too busy, looking up at the sky. He stayed at the wheel, there in the remodeled outhouse, waiting for those who wished to survive with him. His boat, finally, was afloat; it tugged at its lines. The trees to which the boat was moored were themselves surrounded by water. Liebhaber, every so often, abandoned the helm, an iron wheel from an old hayrake; he went into the pelting rain to extend his makeshift dock up the bank. He worked quickly, angrily, almost in despair at the folly of his fellow citizens. When they might have been rescued, they stared with hollow, worn eyes up at the blank gray cover of cloud; they gaped and gawked as if by looking they might hear the mysterious machine in the sky.

It was not until a few minutes after the hailstorm that Liebhaber was tempted to visit all those who were staying on shore. Being soaked to the skin didn't bother him, his hunger was nothing. But the sound of the hailstones, drumming on the shingle roof of the wheelhouse, on the deck of the boat, made him feel he was inside a typesetting machine.

Sitting alone in the small wheelhouse — he'd kept the two-hole board as a bench — listening to the rattle and leap of the hailstones, Liebhaber became quite simply terrified. Waiting, helpless, playing a little pocket pool, he thought of Fust, Gutenberg's coadjutor, even away back then, condemned merely to fulfil what Gutenberg had ordained. He thought of all those admirable men of Caxton, of Jenson, of Manutius, of Garamond, of Goudy. He thought of his own small collection of wood type, hoarded away from the destroying world. Those hidden words, failed in their hiding. Helm. Help. Hell. Yes: his hands wanted those few scraps of wood, those fragments of old trees, carved and cut into the shapes of the alphabet. They were all he had brought with him from wherever the place was that he'd abandoned or fled. The empty brown suitcase on the shelf in his closet, his initials in gold on the rotting leather, was testament enough to a past flight. He no longer remembered whence he had come, nor why. He remembered getting off a train, the suitcase in his right hand, the collection of type in the suitcase. He thought he remembered.

He wanted to take that with him, the collection of type. And maybe the suitcase too. No other reason could have made him leave the boat, climb the muddy road up onto Main Street. That was his only mistake.

Vera's Boy, directing his battle against the sky from the valley's edge, saw Liebhaber leave the boat. It was a stern-wheeler; the paddle wheel was run by a pump engine. Vera's Boy had never in his life started an engine, he had never steered a boat. Years later, when people argued about what actually happened, there were always those who insisted his only intention, in going to commandeer the boat, was to flee. And yet there were others who argued, with equal conviction, that he saw his mother's predicament; heroically, abandoning his own ambitions, he went to his mother's rescue.

Vera Lang, for some reason, had entered John Skandl's granary, on the shore of the river, above the place where the boat was tied up. She'd been there hardly half an hour when the rising flood waters lifted the granary out of the mud, set it afloat. And why she took off her simple clothing, her undergarments as well, that, too, was never explained by any one person to another's satisfaction. But Vera appeared, of a sudden, in the open door of the floating granary. She appeared in the doorway, as naked as the day she was born. She was floating past the town. Obscenely, Vera Lang gestured. She raised up her full breasts, like skeps, like two perfect beehives, to the startled onlookers. She caressed her belly, her own thighs; she let a finger stray into the matted blonde pubic hairs where a few bees, lovingly, clung to the damp strands.

Bees by the thousands followed the drifting granary. They floated on the eddying, dark water; dead or dying or furiously alive, they followed after. Falling out of the limp sky, they found somehow a way to fly; they followed the drifting granary; in the water and in the air, they followed, the thousands and more thousands of bees. The crawling bees on the gray shingles of the roof, on the granary walls; slowly they moved, inexorably, toward the woman in the doorway. And she in her turn gently motioned the bees toward the softness of her naked body. Her face wore an ecstasy of desire and abandon. Her long hands motioned the world, stirred the world into her waiting. She motioned now to the gathering bees, directed the dance and the hum of their coming. She motioned now to the man, her final lover, flogging the black horse through the mud.

Marvin Straw had been watching. He saw the granary lift afloat. He found the black horse that Vera's Boy rode in his dash from the farm to the shore. He hoisted himself up into the saddle, as if into a tree, or onto the crossbar of a telephone pole. He stayed somehow on the galloping horse, he rode through town, past the astonished spectators, onto a cowpath above the flooded line of trees. He followed the shapeless river, his dirt-rimmed eyes fixed once and for all on the naked woman in the doorway of the drifting granary: Vera, caressing the wet bees into the heat of her pubic hairs: Marvin, wildly flogging the old horse along the water's edge. Come to the limit of his desire, he smashed with his two clumped fists at the mare's shoulders — the old horse that should long ago have been dead; he kicked and pummeled the galloping horse toward the railway bridge.

The granary must pass under the bridge. He could let himself fall. He could leap to the floating granary, riding high on the high water. The seedhouse of all Marvin Straw's dark need, the world's vulva and fulfillment in one. The granary afloat, drifting toward the bridge. While the black mare galloped after.

While Vera's Boy, on the boat, spun the flywheel again, got the engine started; and finally he set out, in slow pursuit of both the granary and the mare. Vera's Boy, squatted on the bench, at the helm, in the shingled wheelhouse, the paddle wheel churning. The pump engine firing. And missing. And firing again…He slipped on his sunglasses; he sniffed his nose through the open window.

While Jerry Lapanne, overhead, in his flying machine, circled like a hawk, like an eagle. He was wondering how to land. He must, somehow, find the earth. He came to a break in the sodden air. Jerry Lapanne dipped through a gap in the clouds; he dared his way down, under the terrible weight of the clouds. For maybe thirty seconds, even more, he saw the truth. He was totally exhausted but, nevertheless, he recognized the simple truth. The bridge was no longer a bridge. The flooding river was destroying the center section of the old railway bridge. Jerry Lapanne, in his instant of perception, decided he must warn the woman in the doorway of the granary, the helmsman on the boat, the rider on the black horse.

He saw the granary drifting around a bend in the river, the boat following almost at the same speed. He saw the horse and rider galloping along the irregular line of the shore. Jerry Lapanne for almost a minute perceived the design of the world beneath him. He dipped down lower in his flying machine, to signal his understanding; he perceived that, given the knowledge he possessed, they could all survive. Jerry Lapanne saw that.

Marvin Straw stared only at the woman in the doorway of the granary. Its big wooden skids made it a floating houseboat, the island of his dream, the enchanted palace, the ark of his immortal longing. He did not see the bridge itself, let alone the gap in the criss-crossed timbers.

Vera's Boy saw the bridge. The water was high, too high. He was studying the bridge, wondering how he might maneuver the small paddleboat through the narrow gap where the bridge was broken. His training was all of dens and paths and fields and hunters, not of water. He stopped thinking of his mother. He shifted his sunglasses, against the glare of the water. He did not see the bees.

Vera Lang, if she was watching anything, was watching the bees and the bees only. Their presence filled her with a desire she did not even wish to understand. Thousands of bees floated on the water, flew in the air, crawled on the granary; and she was wild with her first longing. She urged two fingers, quickly, between her thighs.

The black horse saw the break in the bridge. The black mare stopped in the middle of the bridge; Marvin Straw went head over heels, into the river. He was gone for a long time. Marvin Straw was gone for a long time. Then he burst to the river's surface; his head came up shining, clean and strong, out of the water's rip. He swam like a man who had never in his life needed or known water, and yet who now, in an act of creation born of the water itself, invented motion itself. He threshed his way toward the granary.

And Vera Lang reached out a hand. Naked and beautiful and wild with her first desire, she reached a perfect hand to the swimmer. She helped him up into the doorway. In his terror or in his need, under the water, he had torn loose from all his ragged clothes. They passed the barrier of the bridge, Vera Lang and Marvin Straw; their floating granary sailed through the gap in the broken bridge.

Jerry Lapanne, in his flying machine, was trying to signal that the bridge was washed out. It was not a bridge at all. He had seen the truth. He dipped low, out of the air.

Vera's Boy, at the helm of Liebhaber's boat, the window of the wheelhouse open, did not see the bee until it flashed between the left lens of his sunglasses and his blinking eye.

The paddleboat and the flying machine and the center piling of the old CN bridge; at the exact and same instant, they were in collision. They became one. The boat that had turned and was floating backwards. The machine that flew. The center piling of the old bridge, stiff and tall like a lighthouse, in the middle of the swollen river.

41

Tiddy Lang, from the edge of the valley south of her house, standing in a patch of crocuses

just beyond the foot of the garden, witnessed everything. That's when she decided to live for the moment.

Just as she made her decision, a crow came up out of the valley, somehow managing to fly through the falling mist of rain.

"Is that you, black crow?" Tiddy called to the rising bird.

The crow didn't answer.

"Great weather for ducks," she called after it.

Tiddy chuckled a little to herself; she liked getting in the last dig. She went directly back to the house and told Darryl Dish to go down to the river and launch the boat and outboard motor that had belonged to the Adams boy, the chicken thief who had married into the family, to everyone's shame.

Darryl, in his passion for Terry O'Holleran, had forgotten all about hailstones. He was standing at a kitchen window, staring out past the clothesline posts at nothing, one of Terry's hands deep in a pocket of his denim cut-offs. Tiddy had to tell him three times to go, but she persisted, ordering him to go at once and to bring back Mr. Liebhaber. She was living for the moment only, the rest of the world be damned for a change.

Darryl found Liebhaber at work in the print shop, swearing like a trooper, setting type for the next edition of the *Big Indian Signal*. The rising floodwaters were flushing Zike, like a drowned-out gopher, from the basement; he was hauling box after box of soggy, unused calendars up the basement stairs, stacking them in a kind of wall at Liebhaber's back while Liebhaber went on trying to complete page one of the *Big Indian Signal*. Mr. Wills, the publisher, had left the wrong material; he was, as usual, gone off to the city. Make it fit, will you, Leeb? his note said. Zike leaned over Liebhaber's shoulder: "End of the world. End of the fucking world, Leeb. What did I tell you?"

Liebhaber, just to be stubborn, would set nothing about the flood. He made mention, in a long story, of the good fortune that was befalling the community in the form of spring rains that would ensure a bumper crop, after years of drought. He made brief mention of the reeve, Vera's Boy, who'd been so mistaken in his estimates of the weather, and in a box at the bottom of page one he remarked that boating excursions might become a regular Saturday night event along the banks of the Bigknife.

He locked up the form for Zike and went with Darryl to where a twelve-foot aluminum boat, with a six-horse motor, was tied up to a telephone pole beside the Big Indian Hotel. Liebhaber took one look at the small boat and said he'd need a beer before he got into such a tin can. He hadn't forgotten his experience under the hull of his own boat, the day Joe Lightning fell out of the sky.

"One beer," he said.

"Terry's mother is waiting," Darryl said. He couldn't remember Tiddy's name.

"One beer," Liebhaber repeated.

The beer parlor was jammed. Leo Weller was there, pretty well sloshed; the print of the horseshoe, stamped on his forehead, was a brighter pink when he drank. Leo was a pig farmer. He and Eddie Brausen were having an argument about whether or not a pig could swim.

Liebhaber sat down and signaled a slinger to bring six and a juice. He'd once set a story on pigs and had some opinions himself. Then he remembered Darryl Dish, waiting behind him; reluctantly, he called to the slinger to make it eight.

"Make yourself at home," Liebhaber said. He indicated Darryl with a thumb. "This here seminarian is a hailstone chaser."

"You got to be kidding," Leo Weller said.

"No shit," Eddie Brausen said, careful to sound ironic.

The beer arrived and the men drank. They were talking about all the catastrophes there were in the universe when Andy Wolbeck, the station agent, came through the front door. With the bridge out, Andy was sure to have nothing to do for a while; he took off his right shoe and gently rubbed his ivory toes, made from cue balls. Sometimes, on a rainy day, he claimed they actually hurt.

"Vera's Boy," he said. "I was just down to the bridge. They found the body. It was under the boat."

Liebhaber blanched. He poured a dash of tomato juice into a fresh glass of beer. "He couldn't tell rain from drought," Liebhaber said. He wanted to get a little credit for his memory of the future. He just wanted a little credit.

Isador Heck carried a chair from another table, lifting it over bowed heads. He sat down and banged a fist on the table.

"Some asshole ruined my cannon."

Everyone knew that Isador Heck was on the verge of shooting himself into heaven. They thought he was getting scared, making excuses, and they started to laugh.

"Some guy with shit for brains," Heck insisted.

"Didn't do Lapanne any good," Liebhaber said, "going up there." He pointed at the ceiling. He wanted to change the subject.

"Did him a lot of good," Heck said. Heck was arrogant about having flown through the air and looked down on the world. He identified with Lapanne; he believed that he and Lapanne had shared, in some secret way, a vision. He was a great defender of Lapanne.

Jerry Lapanne was found hanged in the telephone wires that were strung along the side of the old CN bridge. He was hanged by the neck; he was found there, purple in the face, black in the face, his blood vessels burst, his neck broken. They had played cards to save him, those same men; they had confronted a mystery that sent them screaming into the streets of Big Indian; they had gone without booze, except for moonshine that had nearly made Bill Morgan blind in his only eye. And now that same Jerry

Lapanne was hanged by the neck. Whether he was innocent or guilty had not made the slightest difference.

Isador Heck was spokesman for a personal grief. "Some total asshole went and ruined my cannon," he insisted. He was getting madder, the more he thought about it; he, himself, a man about to leap from the face of the mortal earth. "Left it uncovered in the rain."

"Nobody would do that," Liebhaber said. He was offended by Heck's sense of absolute certainty. He hated the man for the ease with which he proposed to escape death, absolutely hated him. "How can you be so *sure?*"

"*Somebody* goddamned did it," Heck said. "I'm not blind." He looked at Morgan, at Martz. "I'm not deef."

They started to shout at each other; those same men who had played schmier together through 151 days and nights. Tempers flared. Liebhaber was indignant: no man could be certain of anything on this lunatic, spun and dying planet. Heck was unyielding; he had guessed the way to heaven.

"Invent yourself a flying machine," Liebhaber taunted. "A poor witless jailbird managed to do it."

"I *did*," Heck said. "Some witless sonofabitch wrecked it."

Liebhaber jumped up from his chair and ripped open his shirt. He was a short man, but he had a hairy chest. Heck was on his feet, rolling up his right sleeve off a pale forearm. They were about to come to blows when Darryl Dish said, "I see what you mean."

"What d'you mean?" Liebhaber said. He tugged roughly at a corner of his mustache. The boy's simple remark had somehow unhinged the world. "'I see what you mean.' What do you mean?"

"Who is this smartass kid?" Heck said. He was rolling up his left sleeve. He rolled it down and rolled it up again. Heck had never done anything neatly in his life. "Piss on it," he said. Sometimes he was sorry that everything that could possibly exist existed. "I got to take a leak," he said. "I take it there's no law against *that*."

He was afraid someone would drink his beer while he was gone. Heck was tight-fisted. Ever since losing his favorite team of horses to the barber, he'd been tight with money. He took out his upper plate and dropped it into his full glass of beer. "Liebhaber," he said, muffling his words, "you lay a hand on that p-hucking glass of beer while I'm gone, I'll tear your p-hucking arm off right at the p-hucking shoulder."

The minute Heck was out of sight, everyone reached for the glass. Leo Weller passed it around, from man to man; each took a sip. They sipped carefully, not wanting the stained and dirty set of upper teeth to slide down the side of the glass. Darryl was getting high for the first time in his life. He emptied another glass into the glass that contained Heck's teeth. He took the glass to the next table; he wanted everyone to join in the drinking. He insisted that others take a sip of beer from the glass that contained Heck's upper plate. Liebhaber saw the boy was getting drunk; he began to feel responsible.

"Dumb little bugger," Liebhaber said. "He'll never make it home by himself."

"So he doesn't get home," Leo Weller said. Leo was beginning to feel guilty; it was time he went home and fed his pigs. "What's the difference?" he said.

"He's so goddamned drunk," Liebhaber said, "he's polluted. There's no way he can run that boat."

"Just hope you didn't build it," Eddie Brausen said. He had stopped laughing. He was thinking again of Vera's Boy and how he could, most years, sense the approaching weather. He was thinking of Cathy.

"Here he comes," Bill Morgan said. He'd been watching the door of the men's room with his one eye.

Isador Heck was making his way past crowded tables, through the smoke and the noise, carefully dodging the trays of beer and foam and empties that the slingers whisked through the air. He was coming to claim his glass of beer and his teeth.

Liebhaber pushed back his chair from the table. He called across the room to Darryl. "Maybe we ought to haul ass out of here," he said.

42

There were fish swimming in the streets of Big Indian;

the two men, between them, spotted a dozen suckers and a jack, threshing their way upstream between the post office and Cruickshank's Barber Shop & Pool Hall. Darryl Dish handled the outboard motor while Liebhaber knelt in the bow of the small boat, poking at driftwood with a willow fencepost, testing the depth of the current and shouting the verdict back over his shoulder.

Darryl Dish was happy. All his life, he'd wanted to run a boat. Especially, he'd wanted to run it upstream, against drifting logs and trees that'd been torn from the banks of a river by a raging flood; he wanted to work his way upstream against the current, against the driftwood, against the driving rainstorm, against death itself. He wanted there to be a perfect woman waiting, a woman with child. He'd thought about that, at night, in his seminary room.

Liebhaber felt Martin Lang on his back. He was almost seasick, riding the bobbing bow of the small boat. He was perched in the bow, the willow fencepost raised like a spear, like a harpoon.

He poised himself, balanced himself; he jabbed, warded off a drifting and almost invisible stump. He kept his balance. But Martin Lang was on his back, he knew that.

The boat had hardly enough power to move against the current. The engine was running wide open, and yet, sometimes, the shore was standing still, only the water was moving. Liebhaber's knees were weak when he leapt ashore. He leapt ashore, the painter in his hand. He grinned at Darryl. He raised the painter, held stiff in his right hand. "Saved the day," he shouted.

Darryl Dish was having the time of his life. "I see what you mean," he shouted in reply. He turned his wrist and shut off the engine.

Then they could hear the river.

43

They were barely able to scramble up the slippery hillside, the two listening men,

but they made it, finally, clinging to wolf willow and buckbrush and clumps of sage. They climbed up over the lip of the valley. Rose O'Holleran was in the garden, in the rain; she was holding a funeral for a salt shaker that Cathy had broken. She was kneeling on the wet ground; the pieces of glass and the lid of the salt shaker lay in an open match box to the side of a scooped out hole; the neat, small cross of twigs was ready. Rose was moving her lips in prayer.

Liebhaber and Darryl found their way through last year's garden, under the clotheslines. The sheets and pillow cases and towels and underwear on the lines were wetter now than they'd been when they came through the wringer. Liebhaber went around the caragana hedge, Darryl following. He went up the three steps and across the porch and knocked at the door. He went into the kitchen and found not only Tiddy waiting, but Father Basil too.

Old Father Basil wanted to marry Tiddy and Liebhaber. They should get married, he insisted; and he'd marry them, then and there, right on the spot. On the condition that he be invited to preach a sermon.

Tiddy was impatient. She was living for the moment. "Sermon be damned," she said to Father Basil. "You look exhausted," she said to Liebhaber, "get into bed."

The old priest was heartbroken; he felt that the last trace of the true ethic was disappearing from Big Indian. He hated the young seminarian at sight and was not surprised to see him holding hands with Theresa O'Holleran. She slipped a hand into a pocket of Darryl's denim cut-offs. Father Basil turned away; he walked back toward town, crossing the river with two RCMP officers in a powerboat. He went to the empty church and lit a few candles. He took a sip or two of the sacramental wine.

Father Basil preached a sermon for one hour and eleven minutes. Three old women, come into church to say their beads, or simply to get dry, were delighted to hear the priest in the full vigor of his passion again. They felt consoled. Only when he mentioned the riderless black horse that galloped back from the CN bridge did anyone realize he'd accidentally preached a burial sermon rather than a marriage sermon; for him the two were sometimes interchangeable.

It was the same black horse that troubled Liebhaber's mind. He was sweating in the old, swayback, iron bed; it was probably a mail-order bed to begin with, Eaton's catalogue or something. But it was a bed and he was caressing Tiddy's breasts, touching his tongue to the hard nipple of her right breast, daring to bite, when he thought of the horse. At exactly the moment when Father Basil was concluding his magnificent sermon, a sermon recognized later as representing the pinnacle of his career, Liebhaber was trying to remember the past. The most distant event he could call to mind was his crossing of the CN bridge, on the black horse. With Martin Lang on his back. He felt a fleeting sympathy for Martin Lang; he suspected, briefly, why Martin spent so much time in the Big Indian beer parlor. The pounding of the horse's hoofs on the planks that were the floor of the bridge, then on the road, coincided with the knock of cards onto the kitchen table.

Old Lady Lang, at the kitchen table, was playing hearts with the younger O'Holleran daughter and the three Droniuk girls. It was a rainy day. A rainy evening. When it rained they played hearts, the young girls and Old Lady Lang, around the kitchen table. The knock of cards onto the table coincided exactly with the pounding of the horse's hoofs, coincided exactly with the thump of the thrown ball against the bedroom wall.

Gladys Wurtz had come in from the Hutterite colony to see if she could be of help. Her daughter, Theodora, refused to play cards. Young Theodora didn't believe in card games. Instead, she was outside, in the rain, bouncing a red ball against the bedroom wall. Out in the rain, her red hair going curly, then frizzy, then simply straight, on and on she played, throwing her ball against the wall. She caught it, and threw it again, and caught it again. She hit the window screen. Sometimes the sun peeked through the clouds. Sometimes the clouds, again, covered the sun.

Inside the house, at the dining room table, Rita Lang was writing letters: I want the strength of your hands, holding me. I want the hardness of your cock…Rita, writing. She gave the promise of her words. To her faithful men. And all the while, all her life, she had not opened one letter that came in reply. She arranged the shoeboxes, full of unopened letters, upstairs under her bed. She imagined them all, her faithful men, ripping open the scented envelopes that she so carefully slipped into the mail: Rita, bent at the table, slowly unbuttoning her blouse, furtive and wanton, lifting a nipple to her mouth. The quick flash of her tongue against the rising nipple, the motion of her pen. On and on she wrote, driving her imprisoned lovers to the edge of a terrible dream, a terrible flying.

When the first bee came in at the torn screen, Liebhaber did not notice at all.

Tiddy was living for the moment. She liked the way his body slipped against her own, sweating, his chest sliding over her breasts. She heard the heart thump of the thrown ball against the bedroom wall, the silence again, the held silence; Theodora caught the ball. And threw it again. The old bed, squeaking. The horse, far away, galloping, galloping everywhere. And his words, Liebhaber's whispered wild words, incoherent, his whispered cry: "Here. Hold."

Tiddy whispered. She could see the screen. She saw the first bees, coming in at the broken screen. She whispered, softly, against the subsiding, against the lost demand of his breathing, "Yes?" She whispered, "You liked it…Yes?" She was not asking. "Reach me that towel, Gus."

She liked the slow drip, between her thighs, and the rough caress of the towel, the simple consolation. She liked the tenderness of her love-swollen body, the spent heaviness of Liebhaber's breathing. He was like a little boy. Tiddy remembered everything. She could hardly tell her memory from the moment; all her life, she'd meant to write something down. She'd meant to make a few notes, but hadn't. She remembered JG, shitting himself in the parlor. And she remembered Joe Lightning too, come to the parlor window, galloping in the moonlit night to the parlor window on his proud horse, come to see Cathy. Tiddy was living for the moment. She awakened Liebhaber, out of his first, brief sleep. She aroused him, even while he was almost asleep; she touched him hard with her long, careful fingers; Liebhaber, groaning softly against the loss of sleep, against the return of desire. She took him with her hands, drew him with her warm hands, into the slippery heat of her body. She heard the bed squeaking again, her old iron bedstead, the sagging springs. She'd needed a new bed for years. But now she was living for the moment. She heard the ball, thrown against the bedroom wall; she heard the silence, and in the silence she heard Liebhaber's breathing, his breathing against her left ear; she heard the thrown ball and heard the girl too, and waited; young Theodora, with her nipples the color of gold.

Tiddy liked the coming of night. She liked the silence; she liked the silence. "Helm," Liebhaber whispered. He was a little boy. He held himself close to her body, and in the night he was the inventor of the world's words, "Help." Liebhaber. Silence. "Yes?…Reach me that towel." And he, too: "Hell." The night. Dark. His groping. They were sleeping. All the others were asleep.

The bees were sleeping. The guns were gone from the valley. The rain was only a whisper of rain. He, the having lover; "Ho," his cry, as her mouth found him.

She raised her mouth away from his rising. "Sometimes you're just a little boy." She took him into her mouth again. They lay, together, in the naked circle of everything. Tiddy, then, taking every man who had ever loved her. It was dark outside. The tower of ice, in the depths of her present mind, flared a crystal white. The white tower was almost blue. He had been so huge, John Skandl; he smelled of horses. Her husband was plowing the snow. His arms upraised against the night, against the held and invisible horses, his hair alive in the combing wind. Those same men who had loved her. Liebhaber: "Whoa." And those she had wanted. Yes, the man on the lug-wheeled tractor, on the popping John Deere, riding the horizon, zipping apart the earth from the sky. She had wanted the fish peddler, the eyes of his frozen fish, forever open to the winter light. And the chicken thief. That would have been perfect, the chicken thief, the beautiful stealth of his groping hands. And those she had wanted to want: Vera's fated lovers, the bones of their bodies wise as wine. The gangling man, spun dry and stiff on the windmill; the brute who worked for the telephone company, charging the bull. She is living for the moment. She kisses Liebhaber, hard. And hard. He, the having lover, thirty-three minutes in one best trial. Tiddy was proud of him. "Now," she said. "No." And then she said, "Now. No. Now. Child. Husband. Son. Brother. Old man. Friend. Helper. Enemy. Lover."

And people, years later; years later they will say: against all knowledge, he fired the cannon. He fired the cannon, after all; it was he who dared. He took the bees. He pumped them into the sky itself, rammed them into the sky's night, into the sky's blue breaking. At the mere command of the merest need. He knocked them high, shot them into the one androgynous moment of heaven and earth. He spent the queens into their myriad selves; he, the first and final male, horny to die. The rainmaker, burning the night with the bees' making.

And Tiddy, asleep. She, with no imagination at all, dreaming the world. Liebhaber, finally, understands. She only dreams what she has dreamed. But she is dreaming. He knows now. Gutenberg, too, was only a scribe. Liebhaber, turned end for end in the old bed, his head to the foot, like printers of old, always, reading backwards, reading upside down. They lay, he and Tiddy, together, in the naked circle of everything. His tongue finds the warmth, the heat of her skin, the first small hairs. He sees now the bees. The bees come in at the torn screen. The ball hits the wall. It must be morning. Young Theodora is out in the rain. The bees touch the dreaming woman, touch gold and black her closed thighs. Rita is writing. She flings the words across the page: he is dying, she writes. He is dying in the next room. He is always dying in the next room. She, bent to her tablet, her fingers tight on the ballpoint pen; alone. Alone. All one. A lone. . .

It is morning. Liebhaber, with the slow brushing of his tongue, resists the bees. Rose O'Holleran is opening a grave. She kneels on the wet ground, beneath the tree from which John Gustav attempted to enter the sky. She is in the garden. The rain has allowed her to open a grave. The robin's bones are as delicate as prayers. She raises the small bones; she sniffs the small bones. She lets her tongue touch the beak of the bird's skull. Liebhaber, his tongue to the back of a bee. Anna Marie is upstairs. She sits on her hope chest, on her cedar chest, at the foot of her bed. She watches herself in the mirror. She traces the crow's-feet under her dark eyes. She listens for the children, for Old Lady Lang. Old Lady Lang is in the cellar, breaking the sprouts off last fall's potatoes. Anna Marie picks up a comb.

Gladys is in the barn. She remembers Eli the Hutterite. She is in the loft. She has stolen an egg from under a hen. She lies down in the hay. She raises her long, flowered skirt off her legs. She hears the rain on the roof of the barn, the fitful drumming of the rain. She moves aside the crotch of her bloomers. She rubs the warm egg between her legs.

The ball hits the bedroom wall. Theodora catches the bouncing ball. Tiddy, stirring in her sleep, slowly flexes her knees. Liebhaber folds back the towel.

Vera is gone and Terry O'Holleran rejoices. Now she can have Vera's room. She kneels at the open window, under the slope of ceiling, watching through the screen. The screen is a grid on the garden beyond. Darryl Dish kneels beside her. She slides a hand into a pocket of his cut-offs. Darryl and Terry stare out through the window, through the wet screen, and they do not see the rain. Liebhaber hears the crow. The crow is outside the bedroom window. It is talking, not listening, croaking endlessly on. Liebhaber cannot quite understand what the crow is saying. Perhaps it is talking with Theodora Wurtz. She throws the ball. Perhaps it is talking through the window.

Liebhaber is happy. He cannot remember anything. He rests one side of his head on the towel. He tastes his own semen on Tiddy's belly. He tries to remember the future. Perhaps the crow is telling him that morning has come. He doesn't call out, for fear of waking Tiddy. Liebhaber is happy. After all, he is only dying. Tiddy stirs. But she is only dreaming.

Cathy is walking across the pasture. The cows won't come in by themselves, through the rain. Cathy is the normal one. She is barefoot. The mud and the water and the first thrust of the green grass feel good to her feet. Sometimes she stops to look at a crocus, wet and closed. The crows are cawing. Sometimes she stops in a patch of buffalo beans, stooping to wonder when they will bloom. She is walking across the pasture. Sometimes she does not wonder at all, squinting against the slant of fine rain, trying to spot the motionless cows. Sometimes she talks to herself. Sometimes she looks up at the sky, at the slant of rain, hoping that Joe Lightning will fall into her arms.